Vatican Vengeance

Tom Mohrbach

Published by Tom Mohrbach, 2018.

This is a work of fiction. Similarities to real people, places, or events are entirely coincidental.

VATICAN VENGEANCE

First edition. December 21, 2018.

Copyright © 2018 Tom Mohrbach.

Written by Tom Mohrbach.

This book is dedicated to my mother, June Rose, and my father, Francis, for instilling in me a passion for reading. And, of course to my lovely wife, Cindy, and our daughter, Danielle, who is far more talented a writer than her father. Hopefully, this will inspire her to publish a novel as well.

Chapter 1

EXHAUSTED, FATHER MATTHEW sighed heavily. It had been a long, arduous week, especially now that he had recently celebrated his 65th birthday. After all, he wasn't a young seminarian anymore, and his aching body certainly attested to that. He personally conducted two funerals, a wedding, attended a day-long workshop (about lapsed Catholics and effective strategies to assure their return), coached two CYO softball games, held daily mass, and had just finished the noon Sunday service. He lamented, not for the first time, that he needed a vacation, or a "spiritual retreat," as most priests referred to them.

After properly stowing away his vestments, Father Matthew exited the small changing room hidden behind the sanctuary. Now, clad in the traditional black garb and white collar, he walked around to the front of the altar to make sure all the candles were extinguished.

The odor of wax and candle smoke hung in the air, mingled with the pleasant aroma of dozens of fresh roses adorning the altar. He genuflected and made the sign of the cross at the front of the altar, then walked down the deserted aisle to lock the main doors. He had learned the hard way that even the church wasn't sacred to some neighborhood residents of his east-side Detroit parish, St. Gabriel. Long gone were the days of leaving the doors unlocked to allow a wounded soul to stop in and pray.

Father Matthew's tired, heavy footsteps, echoing off the hardwood floor, were the only sounds within. He was a few feet short of the ornate wooden doors when one side suddenly flung inward. Father Matthew let out a startled, "Hey!"

His eyes widened at the two visitors. Both men were clad in sleeveless black leather vests, with soiled white t-shirts underneath. Their exposed arms were heavily tattooed.

"Relax, preacher-man," said the taller of the two. "No one's going to hurt you as long as you cooperate. Now, where's the little bitch?" His breath reeked of alcohol, despite the early afternoon hour. At a bit over 6' 2" and heavily muscled, the man was a formidable sight.

Father Matthew quickly regained his composure. "Please don't use such language in the Lord's house. No one is here but me. Who are you looking for?"

The taller man nodded to the shorter, stockier man beside him, who turned around and retrieved the long two-by-four that was leaning near the main door. He secured it in the metal brackets, effectively locking both doors.

"No one is going to bother us now, *padre*. I'm going to ask you one more time. Where is the girl?"

"I honestly don't know who you are talking about," Father Matthew protested. "There is no girl here. You can look around, if you wish."

"Oh, we will." The man stepped quickly forward and delivered a powerful punch to the priest's midsection. Father Matthew grunted and doubled over, holding his stomach. The biker looked at his sidekick and ordered, "Find her."

The sidekick stalked dutifully down the aisle, glancing from row to row, as though someone may be crouched down between the pews.

The taller man's eyes narrowed. "Save us the time and trouble. Tell us where she is."

Father Matthew slowly straightened, still grimacing in pain. "If I knew who you were talking about, perhaps I could help you locate her. I minister to many. What is her name?"

"Her name is Allison. She's my little sister. She told me she's been coming here to pray," the man sneered.

"Oh, Allison. I do know her. She's a sweet girl that is very troubled by her brother's life." He said the words a little too pointedly, and when the man frowned, Father Matthew hastily added, "You must be Lucas. I assure you she is not here now."

The sidekick had finished with the pews and was on the side of the church yanking open small wooden doors that led to confessional booths. There was a scream. Lucas and the priest both looked that way to see the short biker dragging a teenage girl from a confessional booth, kicking and struggling as he hauled her backwards in a bear hug.

"Get your dirty, greasy hands off me," Allison protested. "Lucas, make him stop! He's feeling me up."

"You wish," said the sidekick. "Besides, you don't have anything to feel up." This further infuriated Allison, who resisted even more.

Lucas glared at the priest, who stammered, "I had no idea she was hiding there." He delivered a backhand to the priest's face, knocking him into a nearby pew. "Liar!"

"Lucas, he's telling the truth! Don't hurt him!" screamed Allison. "I came in here for noon mass. I snuck into the confessional afterwards and fell asleep."

Lucas ignored his sister's pleas and stepped close to Father Matthew. "Get up. It's time to turn the other cheek."

The priest pulled himself up, gripping the back of a pew. A trickle of scarlet blood leaked from his nose onto his shirt. "Do with me what you will. I didn't know she was here, but please, don't hurt her."

Lucas reached inside his right boot and pulled out a small dagger. He grabbed the back of the priest's neck with his other hand, then pressed the flat edge of the cold blade against his cheek. He leaned in close to the priest. "I should kill you right now. Don't ever allow my sister in here again. She doesn't need what you're selling." Lucas rotated the blade of the knife, so that the razor-sharp edge was against the priest's cheek, and slashed downward. The priest didn't scream, but instead locked eyes with Lucas as blood began to run down his face, staining his white clerical collar red.

"Stop it, Lucas. Please stop hurting him, you jerk!" Allison pleaded.

"You a tough guy, *padre*?" Lucas ignored his sister's screams, his gaze still locked with the priest's. You look like you want to hurt me. Nothing's stopping you. Go for it."

When Allison screamed again, Lucas jerked his head towards the door. "Get her out of here," he ordered. The other biker dragged Allison out a side door, her screams still reverberating through the church.

Lucas grinned. "Just me and you now, preacher man."

"Why are you so upset with me?" Father Matthew asked while holding his hand over the long laceration while blood seeped through his fingers. "I've done nothing to harm your sister. She is very troubled and worried about you. The death of your mother was—"

Without warning, Lucas thrust the knife into Father Matthew's rib cage, precisely where he knew the heart was, and held it there. "That whore of a woman doesn't deserve to be called my mother," he snarled. "How dare you speak of her to me."

Father Matthew's eyes widened as Lucas pulled the blade out, wiped it on the priest's shirt sleeve, and sheathed it back in his boot.

The priest staggered backward, coughing and wheezing as he sat heavily onto a nearby pew. "I forgive you," he said hoarsely.

"I don't want or need your forgiveness, because I don't worship your God. Your God has never done anything for me," hissed Lucas.

Father Matthew coughed again; tiny blood droplets sprayed from his mouth. "Please repent of your sins. Let me release you from them before I die. Let this grip Satan has on your soul be broken now," pleaded the priest.

"No one has any grip on my soul, 'cause I don't have one. There ain't nothing after this life. Sorry you wasted yours thinking there was."

Father Matthew took a last gulp of air, then exhaled loudly, his chin dropping suddenly to his chest. His body went limp, but he remained seated upright in the pew.

Lucas stepped closer and felt the priest's neck for a pulse.

Suddenly, the priest's bloody right hand shot forward, grabbing Lucas' left wrist in a death grip.

"Jesus!" yelled Lucas.

The priest's head snapped upward, his eyes opened wide, and he yelled in a booming voice, "Leave him before it's too late. It would have been better for you had you never been born. Eternal darkness awaits you with unfathomable suffering."

Startled, Lucas yanked his wrist free and stumbled away from the dying priest, who slumped forward from the pew to the wooden floor. Lucas ran unsteadily toward the side exit. As he fled, he angrily knocked over a rack of votive candles. One of them rolled to the wall, igniting a decorative tapestry that read, "With God there is always hope."

Flames licked up the wall like hungry serpents, looking to devour everything in their path.

Chapter 2

THE LONG LINE OF HARLEYS roared up scenic Route 31, two abreast. The highway wound through some of the most picturesque scenery in the lower peninsula of Michigan, alternating between skirting Lake Michigan's sandy shoreline and the many acres of lush national forest. It was a beautiful, early summer afternoon, as waves crashed along the shore. The turquoise blue sky was unblemished by even a single cloud. Dozens of seagulls flocked overhead, looking for beachgoers to harass for food.

The riders were a motley bunch, clad in a variety of well-worn denim and leather. Instead of helmets, most wore bandanas. Several of the Harleys were the classic chopper style. All were very loud.

The procession had passed a few Michigan State Police Troopers on their ride from Detroit to the opposite side of the state, but they were not bothered. Who could blame the police for ignoring them? The caravan stretched almost a quarter-mile long and was comprised of over sixty motorcycles, two vans, a converted school bus, and a large Ryder rental truck. And, if the sheer number of the gang wasn't enough to intimidate, the colors they wore were.

The riders were all members of the Devil's Dungeon, one of the most notorious Midwest motorcycle gangs. They had a long, storied history of altercations with law enforcement; most of them ended with some from each side going to the hospital, and, on occasion, the morgue. The general consensus of the police was to ignore minor infractions—and even some major ones—unless plenty of backup was readily available.

The caravan exited the highway onto a more rural stretch of asphalt. Within five miles of their destination, they drove past an Oceana County Deputy Sheriff, whose vehicle was parked on the opposite side of the two-lane highway.

Deputy Sheriff Matt Toney was running radar. It had been a relatively slow Tuesday, thus far, on his 6am to 6pm shift, and with only four hours left, he had hoped to issue a few tickets to keep the sergeant off his ass. It wasn't as though they had a quota, but the Sarge expected at least a few tickets a day—unless you were otherwise occupied, which Matt hadn't been thus far.

Deputy Toney straightened in his seat as he saw the approaching caravan. Groups of motorcycle riders were not uncommon on this stretch of road, as it was such a scenic drive, but anything over a dozen or so bikes was cause for closer inspection. He didn't like what he saw as the lead bike passed him doing a steady 65-mph in the 45-mph zone, without even a cursory slowdown while passing the deputy.

One thing was for sure, Toney thought: this group wasn't a bunch of weekend bikers on a charity ride—this was an outlaw biker gang. Toney watched them closely as the group rode past. A few riders had women astride their bikes. On the side of the vans and bus that took up the rear, "Devil's Dungeon" was detailed in scripted, red, Old English-style lettering, with orange and yellow flames surrounding the letters.

"Wonderful," Deputy Toney mumbled to himself as he engaged his Dodge Challenger in gear, pulling in behind the Ryder truck that was bringing up the rear of the convoy. Toney was a ten-year veteran of the department. At 34 years old, he was just at that stage in his career where he was comfortable and confident with his job. A sergeant promotion was looming on the horizon.

He called dispatch to report his observation of the large motorcycle gang, requesting that any available back-up units start his way. Dispatch acknowledged his transmission, as did two deputies who advised they were en route, but neither was very close. His duty sergeant came over the radio advising him not to attempt to stop the gang without at least three back-up officers, and only then if they were committing a felony.

Deputy Toney acknowledged his sergeant and hung the radio microphone back on the dash. His sergeant was right. Stopping a large gang of outlaw bikers with only four officers was not a wise idea. That didn't mean he couldn't follow them, letting them know they were being watched closely. "Hostile surveillance" had worked well overseas with suspected insurgents during his stint in the army; why not here?

The brake lights of the Ryder truck suddenly flared as it came to a sudden stop. Toney braked quickly, barely stopping a foot short of the rear of the van. His hot coffee, that he was just taking a sip of from a Styrofoam cup, splashed onto his thigh. "Damn it," he muttered.

They were two miles short of Pentwater and half a mile shy of the closest intersection. Toney flipped on his overhead lights to alert any other approaching motorists that traffic was stopped.

"Dispatch, the gang has suddenly stopped in the middle of the road about two miles south of Pentwater," he said over the radio. "I'll be out checking if there is a problem. Have the other units keep rolling this way."

After hastily mopping the coffee up with a napkin, Toney stepped from his patrol car and looked ahead, unable to see why they the gang had suddenly stopped. Two Harleys were now approaching in the opposite lane. Toney released the safety-catch on his holster and rested his hand on the polymer grip of his .40 caliber, semi-automatic Smith and Wesson pistol. The two gang members circled their bikes to the rear of his cruiser and killed their engines.

Toney did not like what he felt. He had the same sensation on his tour in Iraq several years ago, when he was a Ranger, just before the shit hit the proverbial fan. It was a warning sensation that had kept him alive more than once.

A momentary bout of panic overwhelmed him as he no longer saw Midwestern gang members with bandanas wrapped around their heads, but Taliban enforcers, with their traditional *shemaghs*. Toney fought off the vision.

"What's the problem, officer—Toney, is it?" The taller of the two bikers asked while reading his name plate, bringing Toney back to the present.

"Yes, it's Toney. Deputy Toney. To whom do I have the pleasure of speaking?"

"I'm Lucas. I'm the leader of this band of warriors. Why are you harassing us?"

"Well, Lucas, I guess we could start with the fact you're all speeding, but I was actually willing to overlook that." Toney tried to keep his voice level and calm, despite a hammering heartbeat from a sudden adrenaline dump. His fight-or-flight response was working overtime, but flight was not a viable option. "You tell me—what's the problem? Why are you all stopped in the middle of the road?"

"We stopped because I have to take a leak," Lucas replied matter-of-factly. "We're moving into town. We don't want any trouble from local law, but we ain't restricted to your laws. That makes us a real bad enemy. I suggest we remain friends."

With that said, Lucas got off his bike, walked to the edge of the road, unzipped his pants, and started urinating on the grass. Half of the other bikers, including some of the women, did the same.

Toney shook his head. *Not a great way to start off a friendship*, he thought. All of them were committing misdemeanors in his presence. Arrestable offenses for sure. He knew he had to pick his battles and this one wasn't worth it.

Lucas zipped up and slowly smiled, meandering back towards Toney. "Aw, come on now," he drawled. "It's been a long drive for us. Besides, the state doesn't have enough rest areas open anymore. Word of advice, deputy. Ignore the small stuff, and we won't make any *major* trouble for you."

Deputy Toney nodded, trying to maintain his composure and wondering where the hell his backup was. "Tell you what. I'm a reasonable man, so I'll try to get along with all of you, but don't push the edge too far."

Lucas laughed. "I bet you only have five or so deputies covering the whole county right now. It's a damn shame that the state is in such a financial crisis that you have to spend all day writing speeding tickets and harassing fine citizens." He swept his arm to engulf the caravan. "Look at us, I have over seventy warriors ready for battle. I strongly suggest you stay on our good side."

"I certainly hope you're not threatening me, as that wouldn't be very neighborly—especially since you're moving into town. And, if that's true, we'll be seeing a lot of each other. You'll need to be following our laws or else you will be seeing a whole lotta me. Like you said, let's try to get along," Deputy Toney responded, while staring steadily at Lucas.

Lucas chuckled. "You've got balls, that's for sure. I kind of almost respect that. We'll be seeing more of each other; I'm certain of that." He took a step towards Toney and stuck out his hand.

Toney smiled back. "Sorry, that hand was just holding something I'm not about to touch. No offense."

Lucas looked at Toney a moment, then laughed again. "None taken." He walked back to his Harley and fired it up then roared to the front of the pack. The caravan slowly moved on. The sounds of the dozens of Harley's restarting reminded him of automatic weapons discharging in Iraq several years ago.

Great, Toney thought. *All we need is this bunch of shitheads in our county, right at the start of tourist season.* He sat back in his cruiser and let out a long, slow breath. He realized his hands were shaking and his heart was hammering like a boxer working over a speed bag. He told dispatch to cancel his backup units, as all was well—at least for now, he thought.

Chapter 3

FOUR MONTHS LATER IN Vatican City, Rome:

The underling handed a copy of the most recent letter to Ricardo "The Controller" Mascola, who grimaced. The head of the Vatican's ultra-secret security force dismissed the underling with a terse nod. His usually tacit, no-nonsense nature often rubbed people the wrong way, but his mind was always planning and scheming. He did not intend to be callous, but his position did not allow time for pleasantries.

He quickly read through the letter with a look of disdain etched on his face. This was the sixth such letter in less than three months from the same individual; each subsequent letter contained more specifics, and therefore was of more concern. A man who speaks in generalities can easily be dismissed as a harmless windbag, but this letter's author was cause for more concern.

The individual responsible for each letter had been identified from the very first one. He clearly was not a professional as DNA was obtained from the stamp. He apparently licked it to seal it. He may as well have used a return address. He was an amateur through and through, but he was still a threat. The successive envelopes had self-adhesive stamps, but one slip up was enough. Assassins didn't necessarily require high IQ's. History confirmed that, as many highly capable individuals were killed by the uneducated, especially if assisted by someone more capable.

The simple sketch the suspect made on each letter was what made him very high on Ricardo's personal radar. The sketch revealed the author had all the help he needed to accomplish his goal—a goal Ricardo could not allow to happen. This particular sketch had been used before by other amateurs who were much too close to success to be ignored.

Therefore, Lucas Sledge, a Vice President with the Devils' Dungeon outlaw motorcycle gang based out of Detroit, MI, identified by DNA had now risen to the top of Ricardo's list. A position on this list was envied by no one, and certainly no one that was familiar with Ricardo Mascola and the powerful resources he wielded.

Ricardo sat heavily at his desk and sighed. At times he wished he was still with the *Carabinieri* investigating organized crime. His current position was far more stressful than the days of past chasing down mob bosses throughout Rome.

He pulled open a file drawer and removed a manila folder, depositing the current copy of the letter with the other seven. He lifted his desk phone and punched in an in-residence number. When it was answered by a maid, he asked in his native Italian tongue to speak with His Eminence, Cardinal Lorenzo Colosanti.

Cardinal Colosanti was on the line within seconds.

Without preamble, Ricardo said, "It is time to have Samson pay a visit to the pagan." As always, code names were used, as one could not be too careful when speaking about covert agents and their targets.

"I see. I trust you received another letter," Cardinal Colosanti replied.

"I have."

"And it included the sketch of Botis?"

"Of course."

"Well, then. I concur we must pay him a personal visit. Are you sure Samson is ready so soon after his last assignment? Perhaps we should send Michael instead," Cardinal Colosanti mused.

"Samson is the best we have, and this could involve an entire gang," Ricardo replied. "He is ready."

"Well then, perhaps we should send them both."

"I respectfully disagree, your Eminence. We need one of them here, especially with Gabriel and Raphael still on assignment."

"You worry too much. We have an entire elite guard here 24/7. The Swiss Guard have protected our Holy Father for centuries and very well I may add."

"I am paid handsomely to worry too much. I agree, they are all very skilled, but I still believe having one of the four on hand is prudent," countered Ricardo.

"Very well. Send Samson. Leave Michael here. I will pray in earnest for his success. And Ricardo, please advise him to be a bit more discreet this time. Perhaps remind him of the definition of covert," his Eminence, as usual, hung up without saying goodbye.

Ricardo sighed. His Eminence had no idea what being a covert operative entailed, but that didn't stop him from his occasional rebukes. Ricardo, on the other hand, knew all too well the difficulties faced by a covert agent, but his time in the field was over. He did miss it on occasion. The chase and the apprehension. The hunt, so to speak, was what he was best at, but as good as Ricardo was at chasing down criminals, he knew he was a bit long in the tooth to be in the trenches for an apprehension. The quarry his "Four" were tasked to capture was an entirely different level and breed of criminal than any he ever hunted.

Ricardo walked over to a tall cherry wood cabinet and removed a crystal decanter filled with the finest cognac that his salary allowed. He poured himself a generous amount of the amber liquid while gazing out his tiny window. The dome of St. Peter's basilica filled most of his view. He swirled the cognac in his glass prior to taking a large pull. The pleasant burn of the alcohol calmed him.

He fished his cellphone from his pocket and summoned Colton to his office with a coded text. His memory drifted back in time to almost eight years prior.

Colton Bishop was seated in his office, as was Cardinal Colosanti. Ricardo recalled the bewildered look on the young man's face, a look that inquired why he was summoned here. Ricardo knew that Colton had already spoken with the local Carabinieri; they assured him no charges would be brought against him. Their investigation agreed he was acting in self-defense. How did a skirmish in a darkened Roman alley with five hooligans involve the Vatican?

Ricardo laughed to himself at the memory of how the skirmish started. The five hoodlums certainly picked the wrong young man to rob.

One of the five hoodlums lived in a flat across from the prestigious Roman eatery where Colton worked as a sous chef.

The hoodlum saw Colton leave the fine dining establishment each night from a side alley door carrying a local banco deposit bag. The thug correctly assumed that the bag held the night's profits, but incorrectly assumed the young lad would be an easy mark, especially when it was five against one.

The restaurant's covert video surveillance camera mounted above the door had captured it all, albeit a bit shadowy due to the late hour and poor lighting. The skirmish was over surprisingly fast. From the first flash of a knife blade, and a quick swing of a lead pipe, the unarmed Colton had disabled all five attackers in under half a minute. And disabled was the operative word, as all required extensive rehabilitation to recover from their wounds.

Ricardo assured the young Colton that he was not in any trouble, and in fact, he wanted to offer him a job. Colton had immediately jumped to the wrong conclusion and said it would be a tremendous honor to cook for the Vatican, especially the Pope. Ricardo and his Eminence both laughed heartily at his response, while a confused Colton sat in silence.

Finally, Ricardo composed himself and said, "We don't want you to cook for the Pope—we want you to protect him." It was the genesis of, "The Four." Colton was the last one brought on board. The group was complete.

The memory faded when his underling rang his desk phone, advising that Colton had arrived. "Well, then, send him in," he replied, a bit too brusquely. Ricardo finished his brandy in a large swig just as Colton entered.

Two hours later, after a thorough briefing, Colton, a.k.a. Samson, left Ricardo's office to begin preparations for his assignment.

"Watch over him, my Lord. Watch over him," muttered Ricardo while gazing at the Dome of St. Peter's Basilica. The short prayer was certainly fitting for the location, but rather odd coming from the man who was a life-long atheist.

Chapter 4

ST. MICHAEL'S WAS THE only Catholic Church in Pentwater. It was a small, historic church, almost 125 years old, but what it lacked in modern architecture and size it made up for in classic elegance.

Ancient stained-glass windows ran the length of each side of the rectangular interior. The original rustic, oak ceiling beams were still visible to an upward gazing spectator. The dark walnut pews held a glass-like shine. A large crucifix, imported from the Holy Land over 100 years ago, hung behind the altar, which was a slab of fine Italian marble. Brass gas-fueled chandeliers, also originals, but now wired for electricity, cast a subdued lighting all around. A rich heavy scent of candle wax combined with incense filled the air.

Father Carlos was not surprised to see the stranger in the church, despite the noon mass concluding over an hour ago. After all, his church was in a tourist town; strangers dropped in at all hours of the day. The man was kneeling in the last pew, his head deeply bowed.

Father Carlos had entered from the front of the altar and glided almost quietly across the tiled floor. He descended the three stairs to the main aisle and continued quietly towards the church, hoping not to disturb the visitor. Apparently, he wasn't quiet enough, as the stranger with his head still bowed said, "Good afternoon Father, I hope I am not intruding."

Father Carlos was surprised that this stranger heard his approach. "Not at all, my son. All are welcome here. Is there something I can help you with, or do you wish to be left in solitude with our Lord?"

"Actually, Father," the man who now lifted his head said, "If it wouldn't be too much trouble, could you hear my confession? I'm a bit of a nomad and am new to your town." The stranger spoke softly.

Father Carlos was always a bit weary of wanderers. The man appeared to be in his early thirties and looked very fit, like an athlete. He had thick, chocolate colored hair that hung loosely about his shoulders. His eyes were a riveting bluish-grey, and dark stubble covered his square jaw. There was an edge to his face that suggested a rough life, several faint scars adorned both cheeks, and his nose had the look of being broken once or twice.

"Why, of course! No trouble whatsoever," Father Carlos replied. "Confession is a dying sacrament with most of my congregation, except at Christmas and Easter. I'm Father Carlos."

"Nice to meet you, Father."

The two shook hands. Father Carlos felt a subdued strength in the man's grasp and noted his hands were tough and calloused. "And you as well, Mister—?"

"Colton, Father. Just Colton."

"Okay, Colton. Do you mind if I inquire what your profession is? You have working hands."

"I'm a chef, among other things."

"Well, then, you need to stop at the Riverside Diner just a few blocks down the street. Maggie's been looking for an afternoon cook. Business is slower now that Labor Day is over but I'm quite certain she will be happy to interview you. She has a homemade turtle soup that is simply the best."

"Thank you, Father," said Colton, "but I'm not planning on being in town too long. I'm actually on hiatus from cooking, but I could use a cup of coffee. I presume Maggie is the owner?"

"Yes, she is. A very fine young woman, I might add. So, are you vacationing here?"

"No."

When Colton offered nothing further, Father Carlos cleared his throat and said, "Well, then, let us get on with your confession. Do you want to conduct it face to face, perhaps here in the pew?"

"If you wouldn't mind, I am somewhat of a traditionalist, and would prefer the confessional."

"Well, you have certainly come to the right church. As you can see, we are steeped in tradition," Father Carlos spread both his arms and turned from side to side. "She is a beautiful church, isn't she?"

"Absolutely, Father," Colton replied. "I have visited many throughout the world and can say that although all of God's temples are objects of beauty, yours is a rare traditional beauty indeed."

"So nice of you to say. Come, follow me." Father Carlos led him to the confessional, wondering what type of chef travels the world visiting churches.

When Colton finished confessing his sins and exited the church, Father Carlos remained seated inside the confessional. Never before had he absolved a man of so many violent sins—two of which were deaths, albeit in self-defense, if the man spoke the truth.

What troubled the priest the most was that the man had said his last confession was only a month prior. The sins that he confessed were far more severe than his usual gamut of lust, gossip, and harsh language. Dear Lord, the man seemed such a gentle devout spirit. What in Heaven or Hell's name had caused him such misery?

• • • •

COLTON SAW THE SIMPLE red and black sign in the lower corner of the front window: *Help Wanted*. The outside of the diner was straight out of the fifties: chrome accents, lots of windows, and, of course, neon. The downtown street was lined with trees, their leaves various shades of red, orange, and yellow. A stiff breeze, cooled from blowing miles across Lake Michigan, rustled the leaves, causing many to fall from their branches, not unlike a multi-colored blizzard.

Colton crossed the street, turning up the collar on his tailored Italian leather jacket, and entered the diner. A clinking of tiny bells announced his arrival. He smelled fresh coffee and bacon. Two older men, with their backs to him, were seated at a long cream-colored Formica countertop. They sat on cushioned chrome stools bolted to the floor. They looked over their shoulders at him and nodded.

A twenty-something, tall, sun-streaked blond waitress exited the kitchen, carrying a coffee pot. She refilled the old guys' coffee mugs, then smiled at him. He returned the smile while sitting down on a stool near the entrance.

"What can I get you?" The waitress asked him. He noticed her eyes were emerald green and appeared to take all of him in with a single glance.

"Coffee would be great, for starters," He said without the slightest trace of an accent. His linguistic training paid off.

She placed a heavy blue ceramic mug in front of him then poured piping hot coffee into it. Steam curled up from the dark black brew like early morning fog from a pond.

"Thanks," said Colton. "It smells wonderful."

"It is. Would you like a menu?"

"No thank you. I'm not very hungry."

"Well, now, that's a shame. I have the best homemade food in the county."

Colton was taken aback by the woman before him. He felt an immediate connection to her. He sensed a good spirit within her— not to mention she was gorgeous. A combination of the two may have led him to say, "I hear you're looking for a chef?"

The waitress's perfect smile widened as her face brightened. "Well... A chef might be a bit of a stretch for here, but I could use a good cook. Are you interested?"

Once again, for reasons unknown, he replied, "Yes, very much so." Colton opened two creamers, dumping both into his coffee while stirring it slowly with a spoon. He took a hesitant sip of the coffee. "Wow, this is good."

The waitress set the glass coffee pot down on the counter, wiped her hands on her blue and white striped apron, then extended her right hand to him. "I'm Maggie, the owner. How soon can you start?"

He chuckled, shook her hand and was impressed with her grip. "I'm Colton. Nice to meet you. No interview? No references? I'm hired just like that?"

"We already had the interview. I'm very intuitive. In fact, I should have been a fortune-teller, but my father left me this diner so here I am. As far as references go, if I don't like what I see, or the customers don't like how you cook, you won't last a day. But I have a hunch you'll do just fine. When can you start?"

"Yesterday," he replied with a slow smile, taking another sip of his coffee.

"Great. Finish your coffee in the kitchen. My regular day cook called off sick. The late lunch crowd will be here soon so get familiar with the setup and the menu. I'll start you out at twelve bucks an hour and give you a fifty cent raise in a month, if you make it that long."

Colton slid off the bar stool and walked around the counter. "Sounds great." He couldn't help but wonder again. *What am I doing*?

Maggie smiled to herself as she watched him walk towards the kitchen. He walked with the grace of a dancer but had the physique of a swimmer, wide shoulders and a narrow waist. The two old men winked at her then asked for their checks.

"Leaving already? You guys usually stay half the day," Maggie said. One of them leaned across the counter and whispered to her, "We'll leave you two alone. Should we flip the open sign to closed on our way out?" Maggie swatted him playfully on the shoulder. "You two are horrible, simply horrible."

Inwardly, she wondered if maybe her luck was changing. It had been over a month since Deputy Toney inexplicably broke up with her, and she wasn't getting any younger.

Chapter 5

MAGGIE WAS ON HER COUCH, wearing forest green workout slacks and a matching top, sipping her second glass of Chardonnay. Her television was on, but she wasn't paying much attention to it, as Colton was on her mind. He fared very well for his first day on the job, but her thoughts were more about him than his work performance. She sipped her wine again and felt the tightness in her shoulders begin to loosen.

She hardly even thought of another guy since Matt Toney had broken up with her over a month ago. Her best friend, Amber, had warned her about dating cops and Amber should know. She had dated three of them and none worked out.

Maggie thought it was probably more Amber's fault that the relationships ended, rather than the fault of the policemen she dated. Amber was a great friend, but she still behaved like she was a freshman in college, instead of a woman a couple years shy of thirty. In fact, that was probably what Maggie liked most about her.

Amber wasn't too serious about life. She preferred to live for the moment rather than plan for the future. Maggie, as Amber was fond of pointing out, worried so much about the future she was missing the present and all its opportunities. By "opportunities," Maggie knew Amber primarily meant men and sex. Amber shared way too much information regarding her many conquests of that species for Maggie's taste, but besides that she was a cherished friend.

Maggie had discussed the break-up at length with Amber, like she had her other break-ups over the years. Amber had been her best friend since third grade. They were inseparable, and still were. While growing up they took turns hanging out at each other's home and were closer than most sisters.

Amber was there for Maggie when her mother passed away at the young age of 36. Maggie, an only child, was only 13 at the time, and if not for Amber, Maggie probably would have not made it through that dark time.

Amber currently worked as an emergency room nurse at the Regional Hospital. With a lithe dancer's body and fiery red hair, she was never lacking male admirers. Amber and Maggie talked or texted daily and met for dinner at least once a week. Just three nights ago they were sharing a pizza and a pitcher of beer at a popular pizzeria in nearby Silver Lake, when Amber not so subtly told Maggie that Matt's split with her was probably sexually related.

Maggie was no prude, and enjoyed sex as much as the next woman, but she didn't want to have sex just for sex and told Amber so. Amber had laughed and told her to loosen up and enjoy life.

Maggie wanted sex to mean something beyond physical gratification, and she thought it had with Matt. She didn't give in to him, not that he pushed the issue, until they dated for over three months. Maybe she wasn't as good as she thought she was at it. Amber had many more intimate relationships than she did and made a lot of specific suggestions. Most of them appalled Maggie, but she didn't tell Amber so.

But, Colton was not a cop, so she was one step ahead of the curve. There was something about him. Something other than the fact he was a very attractive, apparently single man. *Apparently single*, she thought, as just because a guy didn't wear a wedding ring didn't mean he wasn't married.

Unfortunately, the restaurant was busy Colton's entire shift, so she wasn't able to talk with him as much as she had hoped, but there would be plenty of time for that. He was scheduled from noon to 8pm tomorrow. Not that talking with him was what she was thinking about. Her thoughts were definitely more carnal. Good Lord, she was starting to think like Amber!

Maggie was secretly glad Colton was pretty much hidden in the kitchen most of the shift, as most of her female regulars would have certainly been all over him. Her afternoon waitress, Diane, was gushing about him every two minutes. Fortunately, she was married, but that wouldn't stop Diane from flirting shamelessly, thought Maggie.

She doubted Diane was Colton's type as she smoked two packs of cigarettes a day, and still had some baby fat left over from her third child. Not that she wasn't cute, but—oh, brother; Maggie was already thinking of Colton as hers. "Slow down girl," she said to herself.

Maggie smiled and took a generous sip of the wine. Her head felt light and her mood the same. This was the first evening in a month she wasn't tempted to grab the phone and call Toney, begging him to come back to her. She just wanted some closure, such as an adequate explanation of why he had broken it off after nearly 18 months, other than the lame explanation of he wanted some time to think about his future. It wasn't like they were enemies—he still stopped in the diner a few days a week for breakfast, or lunch, and they chatted amicably—but that made it all the worse.

One thing was for sure: Maggie found herself lusting after Colton. She thought she would probably make an exception to her rule and have sex with him just to have sex; after all, it had been over a month now. She giggled to herself. She was getting a buzz off the wine. Usually two glasses were her limit on a weeknight, but... *What the hell,* she thought, and poured herself another generous glass.

Her mind drifted back to work. She had to open the diner at 6:00 am and had to be there a full hour earlier for prep work. Colton was scheduled from noon to close. If her morning cook, Judy, called off sick again, Maggie would have her hands full. Wednesday mornings were always busy. Everyone loved her three-egg omelet specials.

It wasn't like she could blame Judy if she did call off again. They had been working short staffed for over a month now ever since Matt had arrested her fill-in cook, Donnie.

Donnie was a decent cook, but apparently was popping Vicodin's like candy. He had made the huge mistake of rear-ending Deputy Toney's squad car while Toney sat at a red light. Donnie failed the roadside sobriety tests miserably, and the eventual blood test results revealed the Vicodin.

Maggie thought it was more than coincidence that Donnie's habit started when the Devil's Dungeon gang moved into town. Matt had shared with her that illegal prescription medication abuse had rose significantly in the county since the gang showed up but finding anyone to testify against them was next to impossible. Hopefully, Maggie thought, someone would stand up to them before too long. Pentwater was too nice of a community for them to ruin it.

Maggie yawned and was surprised to see that the late-night talk shows were already on TV. She needed to get to sleep as she had to be up in five hours. She stood and drained the last couple ounces of wine from her glass. After double checking that her doors were locked, she walked to her bedroom, stripped off her clothes, and slipped between the cool covers. "Goodnight, Colton," she whispered to the empty room, and promptly fell asleep. Her night was filled with naked dreams of her and Colton.

• • • •

COLTON WOKE UP SLOWLY, like a scuba diver rising from the depths of a shipwreck; things became clearer, more focused, as he shrugged off the last clutches of sleep. He smiled at the recent memories of the diner. It felt good to be in a kitchen again.

Cooking was therapeutic for him. He was most relaxed when manning a griddle, a deep fryer, and several burners. The busier, the better. He thrived under pressure. His mind wandered to Maggie, but just as quickly he willed it elsewhere. Maggie was a distraction he didn't need, especially now.

Colton pushed off his covers, stood and stretched. He surveyed his humble apartment that was one of three, located above a downtown laundromat. It was comprised of only two rooms—the main room, and a small bathroom.

The room was sparsely furnished. His twin bed was shoved into one corner, and a mini-fridge with a microwave on top sat next to the foot of the bed. A well-used sofa with a gaudy floral-pattern occupied the far wall, with a knotty-pine chest of drawers with a small TV on top adjacent to it. An oval oak laminate dining table, with three mismatched chairs, occupied the center of the room.

"Home sweet home," Colton mumbled to himself while he padded towards the bathroom. It was clean, but small. No tub, but a relatively new-looking tiled shower. He shut himself inside the small shower stall and was pleased with the water pressure. Extremely ample, hot water was an added bonus. Few things relaxed him as quickly as a piping hot shower.

Stepping out of the shower a few minutes later, Colton toweled off, pulled on a pair of fresh boxers and Wrangler jeans, and returned to the bathroom and vigorously brushed his teeth. He was just starting to mentally plan his day when his thoughts were interrupted by a series of sharp knocks on the door.

Colton rinsed his mouth, then walked over and looked through the peephole. Maggie was standing in the hallway. She was wearing a white cotton blouse buttoned low enough to reveal her ample cleavage. Her beautiful mane of blonde hair hung full and loosely about her shoulders, not pulled back into a ponytail as it was yesterday. His mind began to wander to his bed just a few feet away, and in his thoughts, he wasn't alone in it. He shook off the thought before flipping the deadbolt and opening the door.

"Maggie, what are you doing here?"

"Hello to you too," She relied. "I was in the neighborhood, and thought I better make sure I didn't scare you off yesterday with how busy it was."

"I don't scare easily," Colton said. "Please, come in, welcome to my humble nest."

Maggie laughed "Nest? What are you, some kind of bird? Her gaze drifted to his bare chest and stomach. "Wow. You must practically live at a gym," she said as she felt her cheeks begin to flush.

She stepped into the apartment making certain her hip lightly brushed his thigh as she did so. She surveyed the simple room with her back to him. She was wearing tight fitting black cotton slacks that she knew revealed her well-toned posterior and long legs especially well.

"I try to take care of myself. From the looks of things, so do you. Our bodies are temples, after all," Colton stammered.

"Well, I imagine you have plenty of worshipper," She laughed while blushing more deeply, trying not to face him as she knew her face was beet red.

"Boss, are you flirting with me?"

"Maybe a little. But I don't date the help—even if you insisted," she said with a slow sexy smile, finally turning towards him.

He noticed her flushed face but didn't comment on it. Instead, he replied, "I'll quit now," before mentally reminding himself she was a distraction he didn't need. He was quickly losing belief in that.

"Oh, no, you won't," Maggie stated. "At least, not until after breakfast rush."

"Breakfast rush? I thought you said I worked at noon?"

"Sorry. Judy, the morning cook, called off sick again. I hate to start your second day at work this way, but I need you from open to close. Unless you had something better planned," she said while stealing a glance at his bed nearby.

"Um, no, no plans," Colton stuttered like a high-school freshman on his first date. "None at all. I'll be there in fifteen minutes."

"Make it ten. It's already 5:50. I hope you can cook good omelets. They're on special today."

"Maggie, there isn't anything I can't cook well."

"Kind of cocky—I like that." Maggie grinned. "See you in a few, and put a shirt on, would ya? I don't need all the women customers drooling all over my counter."

Colton laughed and shook his head.

Maggie walked out and started down the hall. She smiled to herself and thought, *Was that aggressive enough for you, Amber?* All thoughts of Matt had vanished from her mind.

Chapter 6

WHEN HE FINISHED DRESSING, Colton knelt on his floor and said a quick prayer.

"Father, I am but a humble servant that deserves none of what you give me. Please help me to complete my assignment here and watch over your faithful flock. Amen."

Colton locked up his apartment and descended the stairs to the street below. On the way to the diner, he passed several small-town staples—an ice cream parlor that had closed for the season, two bars, a beauty salon, a quaint coffee shop, a small hardware store, a souvenir/candy shop, and an old-time barber shop.

Colton wasn't sure why, but he always had a sense of anxiety when he was near, or in, a barber shop. He rarely had his hair cut, and when he did, it was only a trim. Something he would normally do himself. Typically, he kept it at shoulder length. A few different times over the years he had cut it shorter but when he did he seemed tired and weak. His first girlfriend said he resembled the American rock star Jim Morrison. Colton figured it was mostly the hair.

Maggie met him at the diner's front door and turned the closed sign to open as he entered.

"Better get you prep-work started," she said in lieu of greeting. "The Johnson brothers are pulling in. They're big boys, local blueberry farmers."

"How big?"

"Big enough to eat three omelets each, with a side of pancakes."

"Well, okay then," Colton laughed, as he pushed his way through the stainless-steel swinging doors that led into the kitchen.

An hour later, the Johnson brothers left as stuffed as turkeys on Thanksgiving, as did several other customers. All of them told Maggie the new cook was definitely worth keeping. Deputy Matt Toney came in just as they were leaving. He selected a counter seat at the far end, so he could keep an eye on the door. Cop habit—always see who, or what, is coming inside.

"Morning, Maggie."

"Good morning, Matt. Jeesh, you scared all my customers away," Maggie replied jokingly.

"Sorry, I showered this morning and even used deodorant. Maybe they have a guilty conscience about something. How about a three cheese and onion omelet, with wheat toast, and of course, coffee?"

Maggie set a mug of hot coffee in front of him and slapped the order slip on the counter in the rectangular cook's window. Colton, now wearing his hair back in a ponytail, glanced out and caught the eye of the deputy who nodded. Colton returned the nod, then disappeared from the window.

"I see you found a replacement for Tyler," Toney said to Maggie, who was wiping the counter down nearby.

"I did, just yesterday. He came in like an answer to a prayer. He's good. Maybe you won't arrest this one and send him away for a year," said Maggie with a half-hearted laugh.

"I won't if he doesn't give me a reason to," Toney assured her. "Besides, Tyler wasn't too reliable anyhow. Seems like you were cooking half the time when he didn't show up."

"Yeah, I know. Besides, I don't want a pill-head cooking for my customers. Judy was supposed to be here this morning, but she called off sick again. Flu bug going around, I guess."

Their conversation was interrupted by the loud, throaty growl of several motorcycles.

Maggie glanced nervously out the front plate-glass windows.

Toney followed her gaze just as four Harleys pulled into the parking lot.

"Terrific," Toney muttered. "They been giving you any trouble?"

"Not much, but they scare the regulars off and don't tip," Maggie complained.

"Well, we've been keeping an extra close eye on them. Hostile surveillance, so to speak. Apparently, a homicide detective from Detroit is interested in one of them, too."

"For what?" asked Maggie.

"Well, I'm no detective, Maggie, but I suspect a homicide, as it's a homicide detective I'm meeting with," Matt teased.

"I guess that was a stupid question. A homicide... Wow, we haven't had a murder here for a long time," Maggie paused, raising an eyebrow, "Have we?"

Toney sipped his coffee. "Five years ago, was the last one, when that lifeguard was strangled. Anyhow, keep a lid on this conversation."

"It wouldn't surprise me if they were killers. They creep me out," Maggie said, watching the four bikers dismount their choppers and walk towards the diner.

"I'm certain several of them are killers. They're one of the most violent gangs in the country. They seem to be behaving for the most part here, but it's only a matter of time, I suppose, before they cross the line."

The silver bells on the door signaled the entrance of the bikers.

Marcus "The Muscle" entered first. He was followed by two longtime members, Skunk and Whacko, and a probationary, Scotty Williard.

Scotty was a 23-year-old local boy. He was the son of a truck driver who abandoned him, his younger sisters and mother, when he was seven. Scotty's mother turned to crack cocaine to help her through those tough years and never got off it.

Scotty preferred alcohol, especially Jack Daniels. He was a naturally strong kid, and at 6'1" and 210 pounds had some decent muscle on him. He was a dirty fighter and didn't lose too often. He dropped out of high school halfway through his sophomore year. What he lacked in book smarts, he made up for with his mechanical ability.

The probationary members had to earn merit wings, just like fighter pilots, before they could become a full-time member. Today's wing requirement: assault a police-officer without being arrested. Put him out of commission. This was the wing that separated the Devil's Dungeon members from other clubs; even the notorious Hell's Angels didn't have such a crazy requirement of their members.

The first three bikers took seats at the middle of the counter while Scotty continued walking, as though heading for the bathroom at the far end. Scotty had downed a half pint of Jack Daniels earlier and was feeling the rush. Not drunk but fueled just enough for the courage he needed to complete his task.

Deputy Toney watched him approach, raising his coffee mug for a sip. One of the other bikers suddenly nudged the glass sugar container onto the tiled floor. The crash of shattering glass caused Toney to take his eye off Scotty for a second.

The diversion was all Scotty needed. He swooped in fast, delivering a hard-right cross directly to Toney's temple. Blindsided, Toney was knocked completely off the stool landing on his hands and knees.

Maggie screamed and ran for the wall phone, but Skunk jumped the counter and grabbed her. "Relax, sweet-cheeks, and everything will be okay." Maggie smelled his body odor mixed with the scent of marijuana.

"Not so tough are you pig," Scotty taunted Toney. Scotty then followed up with a quick hard kick to Toney's jaw as he was trying to stand. It was like a powerful uppercut punch, but with three times the force. Toney lost consciousness, sprawling face-down onto the floor. Bright blood erupted from his smashed nose, pooling and mixing with the coffee already on the tiles.

Colton flung open the stainless-steel kitchen doors and rounded the counter, striding confidently forward with clenched fists.

Marcus slid off his stool and stood holding both his hands up, palms forward. His biceps were the size of most guys' thighs. "Whoa, whoa, that's far enough," Marcus said. "Let's see if the pig can handle himself."

Colton didn't break stride. When he was within a step of Marcus, he said, menacingly, "How 'bout we see if you can handle me?"

"Who the fuck are you?" Marcus inquired.

Colton grinned. "I'm the new chef."

Colton faked a left jab at Marcus' face while delivering a crushing forward kick to his left knee. The knee buckled backwards, cartilage and tendon audibly popping. Marcus fell forward just as Colton brought his right knee up into his face, shattering his nose. Marcus dropped to the floor, now incapacitated and writhing in pain.

Whacko, who was standing behind Marcus, said, "Big mistake. Now I'm gonna have to kill you." Breaking into hysterical laughter, he pulled a long sharp, knife from his waistband.

"You have a fork to go with that?" Colton asked.

"You think it's funny I'm about to kill you?"

"No. You're the one that's laughing. I think it's funny you think you can," Colton replied evenly.

Whacko stepped over his fallen comrade and swung a wide right arc at Colton's face with the blade. Colton easily ducked it, and while still low, quickly punched Whacko in the ribs, breaking two. He then grabbed Whacko's knife hand at the wrist and elbow hyperextending the arm until it broke. Colton now swept Whacko's legs out from underneath him. He went down hard, hitting the back of his head on the floor with a hollow thud.

Colton quickly stepped over Whacko, kicking the knife out of his reach. It clanged against the far wall. He sprinted to the end of the counter. Scotty's back was turned towards him, as he was still focused on punishing the unconscious deputy by repeatedly kicking him.

He was about to deliver another kick when Colton raised both his hands and chopped them down in a quick, powerful arc, the base of each hand striking simultaneously on opposites sides of the biker's neck. Scott's body shuddered as though hit with a jolt of electricity. A terrific pain radiated from his neck to his toes. He slowly collapsed unconscious to the floor, leaving only one biker still conscious and standing.

Colton quickly pivoted and vaulted the counter. He stalked purposely towards Skunk, who was still holding Maggie. His left arm was wrapped around her neck in a choke hold. He shakily grabbed a steak knife from the counter with his right hand and pressed the tip against Maggie's neck.

"Stop right now, or I kill her. I swear I'll do it," he threatened.

Colton stopped and icily replied, "You guys sure like death threats, but trust me, you don't want to do that. Drop the knife now and you walk. If not, you can join your dumb-ass friends in the hospital, or maybe the morgue."

"I'll kill her, I swear," replied the biker in a shaky voice. Maggie looked at Colton with terrified eyes.

"Wrong answer," Colton replied. He turned around and walked casually back toward the far end of the counter. He again vaulted it and ducked down, momentarily disappearing from the biker's view some twenty-feet away.

"Hey, what are you doing?" Skunk shouted.

Colton suddenly reappeared and leaned his forearms across the counter. He was now holding Toney's .40 caliber pistol that he had removed from the unconscious deputy's holster. The bore of the barrel was trained steadily on Skunk's head.

"What needs to be done, now, drop the knife or die where you're standing."

Skunk blinked several times then looked around at his three disabled friends. Surely this cook was something entirely else, and he didn't want to die. "Okay, but you're gonna let me go, right?"

"Right, but only because I want you to tell the rest of your outfit that I fought fair. I could kill all of you right now. Let them know Maggie here had nothing to do with it. Now, go deliver that message before I decide not to be so congenial."

"So . . . what?" asked the biker.

"Buy a dictionary."

The biker slowly lowered the knife, shoved Maggie forward, then sprinted for the door. Once outside, he jumped on his motorcycle and roared away, fishtailing and almost dumping the bike in his hasty retreat.

Chapter 7

IT WAS A SPECTACULAR autumn morning. Allison was lying on a pine needle bed, gazing upwards through the tall conifers, only a few hundred yards from the clubhouse. The rich earthy scent of decomposing leaves, intermixed with fungi, wild grasses, and sweet pine, filled her every breath. Huge puffy clouds drifted lazily through a sky, the shade of robin eggs. Tendrils of sunlight filtered through the pine boughs, warming her prone body.

A variety of small birds fluttered about the green needled branches, while a red-headed woodpecker hammered on a tree nearby. A lone black squirrel scampered atop a stump nearby, noisily scolding her for invading his home.

Allison's thoughts drifted to her hometown of Detroit, specifically the inner-city east-side area. Allison didn't miss the tough, gritty streets one bit. By contrast, Pentwater was paradise. A small, clean, lakeside community. The dirty brown haze of pollution that usually adorned the sky of her hometown was replaced with clear daytime skies, and unbelievable starry nights. Best of all were the wonderful acres upon acres of national forest just outside the clubhouse's back door.

The abandoned, blighted buildings of her Detroit neighborhood were of no comparison to the countless trails and streams that dissected the never-ending forest, filled with a variety of animals and insects.

"I figured I would find you here," a voice said suddenly.

Allison was startled from her reverie by her brother's arrival. "I didn't hear you coming. I just needed a quiet place to think. I didn't go far."

Lucas was 15 years older than Allison and was her stepbrother, as each had different fathers—not that either knew who they were for certain.

"Relax, I'm not mad, but don't wander off any farther. There could be some trouble today." Despite the early morning hour Lucas was carrying an open bottle of Budweiser. He took a hearty swig of it and belched before settling down in the pine needles next to Allison.

"What kind of trouble?" inquired Allison, who now sat up.

"Nothing for you to worry about. Club business is all." Lucas took another swig of his beer, squinting into the sunlight. "I know you like this place, but don't you miss home at all?"

"Not really."

Allison didn't miss anything about her hometown except her mother, Dana, whom she prayed was now in heaven. She died from an overdose of heroin when Allison was only nine years old. Lucas, who she hadn't seen in over a year, showed up the day after the funeral, and took her with him back to his dilapidated double-wide on the outskirts of Port Huron. Allison had fended for herself since then.

Despite all the bad things Lucas had told her about her mom, Allison remembered her taking her to mass every Sunday and every holy day. She only had loving thoughts of her. Allison knew her mother was far from perfect, but she had done the best she could for them. Allison wasn't about to say that to Lucas, as just the mention of their mother usually sent him into a rage.

"Not really," was all she said.

"Are you sure you don't miss anything?" Lucas persisted. "Not even the Coney Dogs?"

Allison smiled before answering. "Okay, I do miss the Coney Dogs. No one around here makes them like at home, that's for sure."

"I knew there was at least one thing you missed."

Allison had a pang of guilt for what she planned on doing later. She longed for a normal life with a happy family. She wanted to go to school and make friends, attend sleepovers, date boys, and all the other things most teens do.

She shook off the feeling and looked at her stepbrother, "Do you miss it?" Allison asked him.

"A little, I guess. There isn't as much action here as I like, but it is nice to be able to relax a little now and then. Anyhow, I've got to get back and take care of some business. Like I said, stay close." Lucas messed up her hair with his hand, then stood and walked away.

Lucas wasn't nice to her very often, Allison thought, but at times like this he actually acted like a brother. She received some solace from her guilt knowing that these rare good times never lasted.

It was like Lucas was two different people lately. She had read the classic *Dr. Jekyll and Mr. Hyde*, and Mr. Hyde was around lately a lot more than the good doctor.

Luckily, Allison had a two-part plan to finally get away from her brother, and all the evil that surrounded him. It had come to her in a daydream three days ago in this exact spot. She was visited by a handsome man with a confident look and a disarming smile. He assured her everything would be okay if she placed her faith entirely in God's hands. He told her to tell the police what she knew about her brother's murder of the priest, and to seek shelter at St. Michael's afterwards.

Allison was frightened to do that, as her brother would severely punish her if he found out. The man took her hand. She was immediately struck by the most comforting sensation she had ever felt. It was like all of her mother's hugs, smiles, and kisses combined. "I will protect you," he said, and then simply vanished before her eyes.

Afterwards, Allison was so moved by the daydream that she ran all the way back to the clubhouse and snuck into the trailer of Tim "Skunk" Lammers, the only member she considered a friend. She snitched his cell phone and then went to the nearby tool shed, locking herself inside while she placed the call to Detroit PD.

Today was the day she was supposed to meet with the Detroit detective she had spoken to a few days earlier. Surprisingly, she wasn't afraid. She trusted the man from her daydream. In fact, she figured he must be an angel.

Chapter 8

LUCAS DID NOT HAVE his sister's innate sense of direction, and after leaving her, he was lost. What should have been a five-minute walk back to the clubhouse was now going on a half hour. Cursing, he finally glimpsed asphalt, and was relieved to be only about a quarter mile away from their clubhouse.

The clubhouse was situated on the far north end of town, roughly a half mile from downtown proper. It was formerly a restaurant but had been vacant for over a year. The previously foreclosed property was just a tad too far for a comfortable stroll from downtown for most people but suited the needs of the gang well.

It certainly wasn't the impenetrable fortress that their main clubhouse in Detroit was, Lucas thought, but it didn't need to be. Pentwater was the polar opposite of Detroit.

As Lucas strolled along the edge of the road, his cellphone vibrated. He pulled it from his leather vest pocket and grumbled, "Yeah?"

"Sledge, that you?" asked their club president, Ron "Whiskey" Banner. Banner was the only one that called him by his last name. He was old enough to be his father and was one of the few men that Lucas respected.

"Yeah, Whiskey, it's me."

"How are things going over there? You haven't checked in this week."

It was Lucas that had convinced Banner four months earlier that it was time to tap into the casinos on the west side of the state, as well as the colleges in the area, as both always needed what they were supplying. Their Detroit membership had grown in recent years to almost 400 members—more than enough to manage the Detroit area, even with all the casinos there. So far, the expansion to the northwest side of the state was a huge success.

"It's going great. These college kids can't get enough of the ecstasy and the casino crowd can't get enough Oxy."

"I heard the Marauders were trying to take a cut of our heroin sales up there," said Banner. "Nice work with the carjacking from the ferries. Screw 'em!"

Shortly after Lucas set up shop in Pentwater, he was surprised to learn that a Chicago gang, The Marauders, were peddling heroin in the area. Lucas quickly learned through paid informants that it was being shipped inside cars, from Wisconsin, via ferries that traversed Lake Michigan. He soon put a stop to that by carjacking several of the cars shortly after they arrived in Michigan.

Ultimately, he was inviting a showdown with The Marauders, but he wasn't overly concerned, as they were operating in his territory. If it was war they wanted, then he would accommodate them.

"I'm glad to hear you say that. I was afraid you might be upset with me for not running that plan by you first," Lucas admitted.

"Upset! Hell no. I'm no micro-manager. If I can't trust one of my VP's, who can I trust?" Banner replied. "You've exceeded my expectations by far. I admit I was a bit skeptical about the move there, but, damn, you proved me wrong. What about the ladies? How is that going?"

"It couldn't be better. I'm about to double down because deer hunting season is almost here. The hunters might tell their wives they're hunting deer in the woods, but most of their stalking happens in the bars. We got plenty of those here."

Lucas established a steady supply of cheap prostitutes to the area, an untapped market until he arrived. The upper west half of the state didn't support the population or revenue for long term prostitutes, but Lucas wisely targeted the seasonal tourists.

Banner laughed heartily. "I might have to stop up there for deer season myself. How is the recruitment phase going?"

"Funny you should mention that. A new local guy is earning his combat badge as we speak."

"Good to hear. Well, I got to go. I just wanted to let you know I couldn't be happier with your new venture. Keep me posted. I'll talk at ya later." Banner terminated the call.

Lucas neglected to tell Banner that the combat badge was being earned in their own backyard, something Banner would not have approved of, but Lucas didn't care. Normally, when a probationer was earning their combat badge, they would assault a cop from out of town, or even out of state, and wouldn't be wearing their colors. This time, Lucas wanted to make a point with the local law, especially Deputy Toney. He had warned that cocky deputy several months ago when they first met to ignore the small stuff.

The local cops needed to be put in their place Lucas thought. They were harassing his men too much lately. The worst offender was Deputy Toney. Lucas had learned a couple months ago that Deputy Toney was heading up a task force to track the gang, and even, possibly, try to infiltrate it. Toney would learn to fear his men.

Lucas finally entered the clubhouse and slammed the door behind him. Most of the gang were lounging and drinking beers. The big flat-screen mounted on the wall was playing porn despite the late morning hour. Lucas grabbed the remote off the bar and powered off the TV. "Where the hell are they? What is taking so long?" Lucas was not expecting an answer, but he got one in the sound of the distinctive throaty growl of a Harley pulling up to the clubhouse.

A few seconds later, Skunk entered the front door alone, looking harried and worried. The fifty or so gathered went quiet.

"Where are the others?" Lucas demanded.

"Um...I'm not sure, but probably the hospital or jail," Skunk said, with his eyes to the floor.

Lucas narrowed his eyes and walked over to Skunk. "What the hell did you just say?" Before Skunk could answer, Lucas said, "Cause I thought I just heard you say they're in jail or the hospital, but that can't be true, because you're standing here without a scratch on you, and I know for sure you wouldn't leave any brothers behind."

The assembled group collectively groaned, and several shook their heads. Lucas reached behind the nearby bar and withdrew a .50 caliber Desert Eagle handgun. He placed the huge barrel against Skunk's forehead.

Skunk's eyes widened, and he gulped but remained silent.

"Cobra. When you were in the Navy Seals, did you ever leave a guy behind?" Lucas asked a musclebound gang member.

Cobra wasn't about to admit he was never a Navy Seal—although he served in the Navy, he washed out of the Seal program on day one. "Never, boss man. No fucking way," he said, shaking his head. "We never left no one behind."

"B—boss," stuttered Skunk. "Please don't kill me. I couldn't do nuthin," this guy was like Chuck Norris. He was, like, super-fast. He could've shot me, but he said he wanted me to tell you he fought fair and all, and to leave Maggie out of it."

"What guy? Who are you talking about—Toney?"

"No, not Toney. It was the cook from Maggie's. He beat the guys down bad. All of them. I grabbed a knife, and was going to stab him, but he got hold of Toney's gun before I could. I didn't have a choice. He would've shot me dead for sure," Skunk said.

"Slow down. You're talking too fast. Did Scotty take down Toney?"

"Yeah, he did real good. He busted that pig up good, but then the chef came out of the kitchen and did some ninja shit on Marcus and Whacko and Scottie too. Please, Boss, there was nothing I could have done. I ain't never seen a guy move like this dude." Skunk was sweating now, his eyes still fixed on the massive barrel on his forehead. "You know me, Boss. I been with you for a long time. We busted up lots of guys together. I'm no coward, but this guy was going to kill me for sure."

Lucas kept the muzzle on Skunk's forehead. "I'm sorry, Skunk. I really am, but you can't leave a member behind," Lucas said in a strange voice. He cocked the gun. The click of the hammer locking back was very loud in the now dead-quiet clubhouse.

Chapter 9

DETROIT PD HOMICIDE Detective, Dirk Smith, was enjoying the drive across the state while listening to a jazz collection of his favorite artists. He tapped his fingers to the beat on the steering wheel, humming along with the melody. He was currently headed north on Route 31, after having traveled west on I-96 for a few hours.

Dirk thought that his new Ford Fusion rode like a dream. The suspension was as smooth as the jazz he was listening to. He was a loyal Ford customer. It was one thing that the Motor City got right: automobiles were its legacy.

Born and raised in the inner city of Detroit, as well as working there most of his life, Dirk relished a short trip to the west side of Michigan. It wasn't that he didn't like his hometown, despite all the negative publicity over the years. He knew, as only an insider could, that Detroit wasn't as bad as the national media usually portrayed it. A rejuvenated downtown, a renovated warehouse district, and, of course, Motown were but a few examples proving that the city was worth a visit—not to mention world class sports teams, including his personal favorite, Detroit Tigers. He was looking forward to a night game when he returned.

Dirk thought of his upcoming visit to Pentwater. He was anxious to meet with Deputy Toney. The Oceana Sheriff, Clifford White, had informed him that Deputy Toney was the guy to speak with if it concerned The Devil's Dungeon, as he was the deputy in charge of a task force that was recently created specifically to monitor them.

Dirk didn't tell the sheriff too much, as he wanted to play his cards close to the vest at this point. He knew this trip could very well result in his last homicide bust of his career. He was due to retire in a few weeks after a career exclusively with the Detroit Police Department.

Dirk read a passing billboard advertising a local carryout: "Beer, Booze & Bullets." He chuckled at that and said aloud, "What else does a man need?" Dirk had plenty of experience with all of the aforementioned. He had just celebrated his 51st birthday a few weeks back. Although he moved a little slower, and ached a little longer, he was still exceptional at his job.

Dirk's mind began to drift as it often did while he was driving alone. This current homicide case was an especially brutal one. A Catholic Priest stabbed in his own church was bad enough, but to have the historic church set ablaze, as well, made this case a media circus. It went national with CNN within hours, and other national networks quickly jumped aboard. He even got a call from the Vatican when a Cardinal called to inquire about the case and its details. Now that was a first in his career.

Dirk checked his rearview mirror for the hundredth time to ensure he wasn't being followed by some sly media hound. Although the case was four months old, the media still dogged him, as did his captain.

There were very few leads at first—in fact, none. The fire had consumed what little evidence there may have been, such as DNA and latent prints. The church did not have any video surveillance and was located just outside a low-income housing project, in what had once been a thriving business district. Dirk, and his co-workers, canvassed the area, but if anyone had witnessed anything, no one was talking, which was nothing new in Detroit.

Finally, just two days ago, months after the crime, a major break occurred. He received a phone call from a girl claiming to know who had murdered the priest. She told him it was her brother. She sounded credible but didn't offer much in the way of details. She refused to give her name, or that of her brother, until she talked to him in person. She told Dirk she would meet him at a restaurant, Maggie's Diner, located in Pentwater at noon today.

A long horn blast from a tailgating motorist brought him back to the present. While daydreaming he had slowed to 45 in the 55-mph zone. Checking his rearview mirror, he saw the tailgater was wearing a cowboy hat, and driving a muddy black Chevy Silverado with a confederate flag flapping in the wind. "I'm not in Detroit anymore," mumbled Dirk. He quickly let off the gas, pulled to the right shoulder, and jammed on his brakes.

The driver of the Silverado veered hard to the left, narrowly missing the rear of the Ford. The enraged cowboy blared his horn and flipped the bird at the lone black man as he passed. Dirk was holding a gold police badge in his left hand, and a handgun in his right with the barrel pointed upwards. The driver of the Silverado quickly lowered his middle finger and mouthed, "Sorry."

"If you don't respect the man, you best respect the gun and badge, you redneck asshole," Dirk said angrily to himself. He drove back onto the highway passing a road sign: Pentwater, 15 miles.

Chapter 10

COLTON TOLD MAGGIE to call 911. She didn't move, looking as if she were staring through him. He knew she was in the beginning stages of shock. He would have to tend to her later, as Deputy Toney, was his immediate priority.

Colton knelt beside the deputy and grabbed the radio microphone that was attached to his shirt collar. Glancing at Toney's nameplate, he said into the radio, "Officer down, officer down at Maggie's Riverside Diner!"

A reply was immediate. "This is Dispatcher three. To whom am I speaking?" inquired a surprisingly calm, female voice.

"I'm the chef here. Deputy Toney is badly injured. He was attacked by bikers with the Devil's Dungeon. He is breathing but not conscious. He appears to have a broken nose, ribs, and, I'm guessing, a concussion at the minimum. We need an ambulance right away."

"Okay, sir. I am sending additional police units and an ambulance your way. Are the attackers still there?"

"Yes, but they are temporarily incapacitated and will require medical attention as well." Colton was trying to calm himself with focused breathing while the adrenaline dissipated from his bloodstream.

"What is the extent of their injuries?"

"They'll live," Colton replied.

Colton removed Deputy Toney's handcuffs from the leather case attached to his duty belt and walked over to the prostrate figure of the probationary biker, who was beginning to come around. Colton snapped a cuff on the biker's left wrist and dragged him across the tile floor to the other two bikers.

Marcus, "The Muscle," was holding his knee, still moaning in pain while writhing on his side on the cold tile floor.

"Man up a little," Colton said to him. "You're supposed to be tougher than that."

"You're a dead man," Marcus snarled.

"Really? I feel great, how about you?"

Colton dragged the probationary past Marcus a few feet and slapped the other cuff to the right wrist of Whacko, who was attempting to stand up.

Colton shoved him roughly downward, "Stay down." The biker cursed as a jolt of fresh pain flared through his side when he hit the floor.

Colton walked around the counter to Maggie, who was slumped on the floor in a seated position. He knelt before her, taking her face in his hands. "It's okay," he said. "Everything is okay now. The deputy will be fine in a few days. Breathe in deeply through your nose and exhale through your mouth," Colton gently instructed and demonstrated how he wanted her to breathe.

After Maggie completed a few cycles of the breathing, he lowered his hands and gently helped her stand, then guided her to a seat near the register. Pouring her a cup of coffee, he said, "Drink this. It'll help." Maggie took a hesitant sip. Tear's leaked from her eyes, trailing down her cheek.

"Why . . . why would anyone do that to him? He didn't do anything to them. How did you do that—that stuff you did?"

Colton heard sirens in the distance. "We'll talk later. Just try to breathe nice and deep and slow."

Colton got some ice from the freezer, wrapped it in a towel, and walked back to Deputy Toney. He placed the towel against the deputy's face, which was puffing up like a blowfish.

Two squad cars suddenly slid sideways into the parking lot with their lights and sirens activated. Seconds later, two deputies raced inside with their handguns drawn. They looked at Maggie, then the three bikers on the floor. Colton slowly stood up from next to deputy Toney's inert body, with his hands held high. "It's okay. I'm a chef here. Maggie is in a bit of shock. Your friend will be okay."

The older of the two deputies trained his Smith & Wesson .45 on Colton and said, "Move slowly away from him. Kneel and face away from us. My partner is going to cuff you until we figure this out."

"I understand." Colton did as instructed and was immediately handcuffed by the younger deputy.

The bells on the entrance door jingled, and everyone turned to face to the door. A middle-aged, bald, black man dressed in a casual suit raised his hands slowly as the older deputy trained his handgun on the stranger.

"Easy, officers, we're on the same team," said Detective Dirk Smith, "I'm a Detroit PD homicide detective. I'm not sure what has happened, but I certainly hope it didn't involve a teenage girl."

Chapter 11

ALLISON STOOD UP FROM her favorite spot in the pines, brushing the needles off her jeans. Her stomach was gurgling, telling her what she already knew: she was starving. Hopefully, the Detroit detective would buy her lunch.

She said a quick prayer that her brother would be busy and not notice her missing for so long. It wasn't like he never let her wander, or leave the clubhouse, but if he knew what she was about to do ... She shuddered at the thought.

Allison continued praying while she walked towards the diner, hoping for the courage to speak with the Detroit PD Detective. She glanced nervously at her gold and silver watch. It was the only memento she had left from her mother. She knew not many teenagers wore watches anymore, as most had cell phones to tell time by, but Lucas didn't allow Allison to own a phone. It was almost noon. What if the detective didn't come? What if he didn't believe her? What if he arrested her? All these thoughts worried her, and she quickened her pace, not wanting to be late for the meeting.

Allison pushed those thoughts from her mind by remembering her mother's funeral, recalling how her mother looked so peaceful in the casket, clutching the single red rose. The wake was sparsely attended as her mom was an only child, and both of her parents had already passed away. If not for a well-to-do, enigmatic uncle, her mother would have had a pauper's funeral.

Uncle Jim lived in Los Angeles. He was some sort of movie producer but did fly out for the funeral. He apologetically explained he wasn't in a position to raise her, and being unable to locate Lucas, placed her in foster care.

Lucas showed up a few days after the funeral and kidnapped her from the foster family. She often wished he had not come back for her. She wondered how her life would have been different. She asked him recently why he took her away from them, and he told her that it was because she was the only family he had left.

A large doe bolted from a nearby thicket a few feet away. The sudden sound, and quick movement in the otherwise quiet woods, startled Allison causing her to jump backwards and scream. She laughed at herself before continuing.

Allison stayed in the woods all the way until town, walking the subtle deer trails as though they were sidewalks. She had certainly adapted to her new environment quickly. She purposely avoided the roads in case one of the club members was out and about. They would question where she was going, or, worse yet, tell her brother she was out wandering without his permission. She felt like Judas about to betray Jesus, but her brother was certainly no Jesus.

She carefully made her way towards the main roadway through town and peered cautiously through the colorful foliage at Maggie's Diner, less than a hundred yards away. Her heart sank, and her stomach went sour. The diner was surrounded by a half dozen police cars with their overhead lights on. Besides the uniformed policeman, she saw a bald black man inside the diner talking with several deputies. He had a gold badge affixed to his suit coat pocket. She correctly guessed he was Detective Smith from Detroit.

Obviously, the detective wanted to arrest her, no doubt telling the local cops all about her. They would certainly arrest her upon sight. Why else would all the police be there?

Tears began to roll down her cheeks as she suddenly realized how today was not the day, she would finally be free from her brother. She watched a moment more, then turned from the roadway and ran deeper into the woods, before collapsing to her knees and sobbing. She eventually found the strength to stand but cried softly the entire walk back to the clubhouse.

She felt completely and utterly alone. Where was her angel now? Maybe it was all just a daydream. After all, why would an angel appear to her? She was just a stupid kid. She wasn't anyone special—far from it. She was foolish to believe God loved her. How could He when she had not told anyone about her suspicions that her brother had killed a priest until just a few days ago. She knew she should have reported him immediately, but she had been a coward.

It was dumb of her to think the police would help her. They were probably going to charge her as an accessory, she thought. She knew they did that from all the cop shows on television. Now, not only was her brother going to be arrested but she as well. She couldn't imagine a life in jail. The confinement was horrifying to her. She loved exploring and wandering. Her pace slowed as a realization entered her racing mind. Ending her life was the only way out of this mess. And, if she was doomed to Hell, then so be it, as she felt like she was in Hell already, living with her brother and his group of degenerates.

She made up her mind that she was going to hang herself. It would probably be painful, but she figured not for long. She wanted to have her favorite picture of her mother with her when she did. It was from her fifth birthday. She thought back to the moment it was taken—her mother bent over her, they were cheek to cheek, smiling widely. A round chocolate cake was before them, five pink candles burning in its center.

Allison approached the rear of the clubhouse and entered quietly. She immediately heard her brother arguing with someone in the bar area. He sounded furious. She tiptoed to her room but continued silently down the hallway towards the main lounge. As she neared the end of the hallway, she kneeled and peered carefully around the corner, just like the cops did on TV.

She saw Lucas holding a gun to Skunk's forehead. Skunk was the only member of the gang that Allison remotely cared about besides her brother. He actually was nice to her. He was one of the few guys that didn't leer at her or make suggestive remarks. Skunk was pleading for his life. A second later, Lucas pulled the trigger.

Allison recoiled in horror as the back of Skunk's head separated from the rest of him. Her eyes were impossibly wide. She took a step into the bar area. Lucas, still holding the gun, saw her. She silently held his gaze a moment before clenching her fists and screaming, "I hate you. You ruined my life. You're a murderer. I hope the cops kill you!"

Before he could respond Allison turned and ran down the hallway, darted into her room and grabbed the picture from the nightstand before continuing out the back door. She scooped up a coiled, heavy duty, electrical extension cord from the sidewalk before sprinting back into the woods.

After running for more than a mile, she doubled over and vomited onto the ground. She scooped up a handful of fallen leaves and wiped her mouth. Her breathing came in ragged gasps. Before her was a tall oak tree. She shakily stood, stomped determinedly towards it, and began to climb with the extension cord looped over her shoulder.

She reached a branch, about 20 feet from the ground, that she was able to scoot out onto. The extension cord was only 12 feet, so she reasoned she was plenty high enough. Crying now, she cinched the cord around the branch she was seated on, then tied the other end around her neck using a slip knot. Sobbing, Allison said a quick prayer asking God to reunite her with her mother and started to lean forward.

Chapter 12

"ALLISON, WAIT!" LUCAS yelled as his sister ran down the hall, "aw shit." His voice and the moaning of the actors from the porn flick still playing on the television, were the only sounds in the room. The other members were still in shock, but he sensed their disapproval. Lucas knew he had crossed the line. Skunk was—had been—a respected, long-time member. It wasn't unusual for a vice president to have to discipline a member, but discipline normally was a loss of rank or club privileges, certainly not execution. Lucas couldn't believe he pulled the trigger. It was as if someone else did. He actually liked Skunk.

Lucas knew he had to assert confidence and control fast, "I made an executive decision. I know it isn't a popular decision, but we simply can't leave an injured member behind. There is no way I can condone that. I liked Skunk as much as the rest of you did," he said, while still wondering why he had acted so rashly. It was the same feeling he had when he killed the priest in Detroit. He was angry then but not so much as to stab him like he did.

Lucas slowly let his gaze linger about the room trying to take in everyone. He saw indecision and disdain on their faces. He knew he needed to continue his justification of what he did.

"Hell, I recruited him after all. He fucked up really bad, and if I screw up that bad, someone better put a bullet in my head. Now, we got some work to do. Spider and Knuckles get that roll of carpet from the back shed and wrap Skunk up in it. We'll bury him out back in the woods after dark."

Lucas pointed at one of his enforcers and said, "Sack. You pick some other guys and go find that cook and bring his ass back to me—alive."

Nobody moved. Furtive glances were exchanged among the members. Lucas glared about the room and stated, "You all deaf or something? Move your asses."

Sack slowly stood and locked eyes with Lucas and said, "You shouldn't have killed him. That wasn't right. I mean, we all know he screwed up bad, but putting a bullet through his brain? Decisions like that should go through the council and president."

Lucas stared at Sack while still clutching the huge pistol, the barrel now pointed at the floor. He knew he was on the verge of losing command. Sack was one of the toughest guys he had and would love to be Vice President. Lucas could not risk a mutiny.

"Are you questioning my leadership, Sack?" Lucas snarled.

"No, but I am questioning the decision you made to kill Skunk."

"Sounds like the same thing to me. I'll tell you what," Lucas said, as he cocked the hammer back on the gun again and took a few steps towards him with the barrel still pointed at the floor. Sack defiantly stood his ground. Lucas raised the gun, and pivoted the grip in his hand, so that the butt of the huge weapon faced Sack." Go ahead. Take it," he said. Sack hesitated. "I said take the damn gun!" ordered Lucas. Finally, Sack did so.

"Shoot me if you think I made the wrong decision."

Sack slowly raised the huge handgun and pointed it at Lucas. The two locked eyes for several seconds. When Sack didn't shoot, Lucas leaned his forehead against the end of the barrel and said, "Do it. Shoot me if you believe that's what needs to be done."

Sack blew out a long, slow breath and lowered the gun to his side, "Damn, Lucas, you're a crazy bastard, but I still respect you. You have always been fair in the past, but damn, I'm still not okay with what you did; I doubt most of us are, but I'm not gonna shoot you for it."

Lucas smiled and patted Sack on the shoulder before taking his gun back. "Okay, then. We can disagree on things. Your opinion is noted. Now, get some guys and go find me that damn cook before I decide to shoot someone else."

That got them all moving.

Chapter 13

IT WAS A LONG DAY. Maggie closed the diner after the attack and drove Colton to the Sheriff's Department, which was located centrally in the county several miles east of Pentwater.

They were interviewed separately for over an hour and asked to provide written statements as well. It was during the interviews that Colton learned Maggie and Deputy Toney had dated for over a year. He felt a twinge of jealousy when he learned this.

Afterwards, Maggie told him she was going to the hospital to check on Deputy Toney. Colton offered to accompany her. Maggie quickly accepted his offer. She stared intently out the front window while driving, barely speaking to him. Colton figured she was still suffering from the residual effects of shock.

"You ok?" Colton inquired, "Would you like me to drive?"

"I'm fine. I'm just worried about Matt. Why would they do that to him? I mean especially in my diner with us as witnesses?"

"It's a classic gang approach. They're trying to establish dominance through intimidation. They wanted witnesses. They wanted you to spread the word about how tough they think they are. They thought you would be too frightened to make a statement to the police," Colton answered.

"Well, thanks to you, that plan didn't work out so well for them, did it?" Maggie answered.

"No, I guess not, but they were expecting your usual cook, not me."

Maggie laughed softly and said, "I guess Matt and I were lucky that Judy called off sick this morning. God knows what would have happened if she was there instead of you."

"I don't think luck had anything to do with it," Colton replied.

"Fate, I guess. Do you think they would have killed Matt if you hadn't intervened?" Maggie asked.

"I doubt it. If they wanted to kill him, they would have shot him. I think it was probably an initiation. The guy beating on the deputy looked younger than the others."

"I know him. He's a local kid that joined up with those bastards about a month after they came to town. He's always been a loser. Matt's busted him before a couple times for petty theft and stuff like that."

"That makes sense. He's earning his way into their confidence," Colton mused.

"So, you and Matt were dating?" Colton asked, hoping to sound casual about it, but failing miserably. He then quickly added, "The detective interviewing me mentioned that," *Stop talking stupid* Colton thought to himself.

Maggie took her eyes off the road for a few seconds and scrutinized Colton. He was looking forward but felt the weight of her stare. After about a minute she said. "We were, but he broke up with me over a month ago. I guess we just didn't click. He still stops in the diner a few times a week. It's kind of strange, I guess," Maggie offered.

Colton didn't say anything as he didn't know how to respond and was sorry he said what he did. He reminded himself to stay on track. Keep focused on his work. Fortunately, Maggie broke the awkward silence by saying, "Here we are."

The hospital loomed in front of them—a sprawling, large, two-story, brick-and-glass building with a huge, oval lawn in front. Maggie pulled her car into the Emergency lot and jerked it into a parking space. Colton, politely, didn't comment on her bouncing the tires off the curb.

They walked silently across the lot and into the emergency room. Once inside they learned from an elderly information booth attendant, that Deputy Toney had been moved to ICU. They rode an elevator up to the second floor and walked towards Toney's room. The smell of mild disinfectant and other chemicals filled the air.

Two deputies were standing guard outside of his room. A handsome, young doctor in blue scrubs was just walking out of the room, reading his clipboard. He practically ran into them. He smiled when he saw Maggie, as did the deputies.

"He's going to be ok, Maggie," offered the doctor.

"How bad is he?"

"Well, he suffered a fractured left orbital and nose, two fractured ribs, a concussion, severe contusions about his torso and legs, and had a rear molar knocked out, but all in all, as bad as that sounds, he should be back to work in a month or so. He's a tough guy and in great shape," the doctor replied.

"Can I see him?"

"Sure but keep it brief; he needs to sleep and is doing so now. Don't worry, he is in good hands." The doctor smiled, then looked expectantly at Colton.

"Oh, I'm sorry. This is Colton, my new cook. Colton, this is Dr. Findlay."

"Are you the same cook that put three of the deputy's attackers into our hospital?" Dr. Findlay asked incredulously.

"Um, yeah, that was me. Sorry," Colton apologized.

"I expected someone bigger, um, more thuggish looking."

Colton laughed, "I get that a lot."

"You put people into the hospital often?" The doctor asked, now sounding serious.

Colton didn't say anything. Maggie looked curiously at him then quickly interjected, "He saved Matt's life and mine too."

"Well, then I'm glad he was around. I better get to my other patients. It was nice meeting you Colton; and Maggie, I'm still single, you know."

Maggie shook her head. "I know, you won't let me forget."

"Well, you can't blame a guy for trying," he countered.

She smiled at him, then turned and entered Toney's room. Colton followed a step behind. Matt was heavily sedated and was sleeping deeply. Maggie took hold of his hand. Two IV's ran into his arm. His face was partially bandaged. The only sound was a gentle humming and beeping from the machines monitoring his vitals. After a few minutes, Maggie bent over and kissed Toney tenderly on the cheek, whispering for him to get better soon. She wiped a trail of tears from her face and abruptly turned away. Colton was surprised when she took hold of his hand and led him out of the room.

The same two deputies, who had initially responded to the diner, were now standing outside in the hall, chatting with the other deputies that were standing guard. They all shook Colton's hand. The older deputy said, "Nice job in the diner. You did really good there."

Colton deflected the praise stating that anyone would have done the same thing. Maggie had piped up that no one could have done what he did.

"Where did you learn to defend yourself? I'm guessing Army Special Forces?" inquired the older deputy.

"Nothing that demanding, just some Jujitsu during my upbringing," Colton partially lied. Jujitsu was only a small part of his extensive training.

"Hmm, well we have a reserve deputy program; if you're interested, I can get you in. We could use a guy like you."

"Thanks, but I think I'll stick to cooking—less stress."

"I don't know about that; I watch that Ramsey guy on TV, and he is always under stress," the deputy said.

Colton laughed, "Yes, he certainly is. Actually, in person, away from the cameras, he's a real serene guy."

"You met him?" asked the younger deputy.

"A couple times. I even cooked for him once, and he actually liked it."

"Wow—I'll buy you a beer some night, and you can tell me about that," offered the young deputy.

The older deputy then said in a more serious tone, "Watch your back. Those losers will be looking for payback, and they won't fight fair. We'll keep regular patrols by the diner and your apartment building."

"Thanks, I'll be fine, but please keep an eye on the diner and Maggie's place."

"I would certainly appreciate that," added Maggie.

Colton and Maggie said goodbye to the deputies and walked down the sterile, white hall towards the elevators. They rode down in silence. As soon as they stepped out, an attractive redheaded nurse rounded a corner wearing green scrubs that appeared to have been tailored to fit her many curves.

"Maggie!" She squealed and ran to her. They hugged fiercely. The nurse told Maggie not to worry that she would take good care of Matt. When they separated, she looked at Colton and smiled widely.

"Don't even tell me this is your new cook. If he is, I'm ordering takeout, and I want him to deliver," she said to Maggie, talking as though Colton wasn't even there, while her eyes appraised every inch of him.

Colton held out his hand and said, "I'm Colton, and yes, I'm the chef, but sorry we don't deliver. Do we?" asked Colton while looking towards Maggie.

"No, we don't," Maggie said a bit too quickly and sternly.

She shook Colton's hand a bit longer than normal and said, "I'm Amber, Amber Weber. If you don't deliver, maybe you should injure yourself, and I could nurse you back to health; but, from what I hear, that probably doesn't happen too often. The deputies are talking about you with awe."

"I apologize for my friend," Maggie said. "She wouldn't feel right if she didn't flirt with every man she meets," Maggie said this in a less than favorable manner. "Anyhow, we have to go. It has been a long day." Maggie grabbed Colton's hand for the second time and started guiding him toward the exit doors.

Amber stared after them and now realized why Maggie hadn't mentioned her new cook to her. Perhaps Maggie would finally get over Matt.

As they exited the hospital, the reddish sun was low on the horizon. Its rays were getting cooler. Sunset was less than a couple hours away. Maggie handed Colton the keys to her silver Honda Accord as they approached it, "Can you drive us back? I'm exhausted."

"Sure."

Colton hit the remote opener and slid in behind the driver's seat of the Honda Accord. He hit the switch to reverse the seat back to a comfortable length and started the car. As he backed out of the space, he thought about the exchange between Maggie and Amber and smiled to himself.

They drove on in silence for a few minutes, then Maggie asked, "Where did you learn to fight like that?"

Colton adjusted his rearview mirror, "the Internet."

"Yeah, right," Maggie said and playfully punched him on the shoulder.

"Ouch," Colton cried.

"Seriously, you were really something. Tell me," she pleaded.

Colton was quiet a moment deciding how much to share. "It's a long story but I've been learning to fight my whole life. I've always been intrigued by really good fighters; boxers, martial artists, wrestlers, gladiators, all those styles of fighting."

"Well, we have a long drive back to town, and this sounds like it will be a very interesting topic."

"Maybe another time boss. I'm kind of tired too. Not much in the mood for talking."

"Please, call me Maggie. Boss sounds so old." She leaned over the center console and kissed him tenderly on the cheek. "Thank you for all you did today. You saved my life and Matt's as well. Maggie rested her head against his shoulder. Her soft blond hair felt good on his neck. He could smell the light citrus scent of her shampoo.

Colton suddenly felt a visceral longing for this woman next to him. Not just a physical sensation, but a connection on an emotional, almost spiritual level as well. Maggie now placed her hand on his right thigh. They drove on in silence for a few minutes. Colton mentally warned himself once again to be careful, not to get too involved.

Maggie slowly lifted her head from his shoulder and softly called his name. He turned to look at her. She leaned forward, her lips softly pressing against his. He kissed her tenderly. She opened her lips wider and started to kiss him hungrily. Her hand on his leg now squeezed his strong thigh muscles. He, involuntarily, jerked the car to the left, then corrected it back to the right, their embrace now broken.

She laughed. It sounded like music to him.

"You about killed us," he said.

"But you would have died with a smile on your face," she said.

Colton was about to reply when a sudden roar of loud exhausts surprised them as three Harleys roared past the car, then cutting abruptly back into their lane and slowed.

"This isn't good," said Colton, as he hit his brakes slowing the car from 50 mph to 30.

Maggie glanced behind them and saw four more bikes behind them. "It sure isn't. What are we going to do?"

"It depends on what they have in mind," replied Colton.

Maggie was shocked how quickly Colton's entire demeanor had changed. His voice was confident, but cold. The passionate, kind man of seconds earlier was gone.

"I'll call 911," offered Maggie as she reached into her purse for her cell.

'No, don't do that. We don't need more deputies getting hurt."

"Colton, what about us?" she asked incredulously, "These guys mean business."

"So do I," Colton replied icily.

The stretch of highway was between two towns with minimal traffic. Colton lifted his foot from the accelerator. "Hold on," he said, before abruptly turning down an isolated, dirt road that led into the woods, the suspension of the car protesting audibly as it bounced up and down along the rutted road.

"Colton, what are you doing? Where are you going?" Maggie asked while bracing her left hand on the roof of the car and her right on the seat.

The four bikes that were following stayed with him. The three others that had been ahead of them quickly U-turned and joined the others, following the car deeper into the forest.

"I want to get away from the main road."

"Why would you want to do that?" Maggie asked with obvious exasperation in her voice.

"To show them I'm not afraid of them, and to assure that no one interferes with us."

Colton suddenly jammed on the brakes. The car slid to a sudden stop. "Do not get out of this car, no matter what. Stay inside."

Maggie grabbed his right arm as he opened the door with his left, "Colton, please don't do this. There are seven of them!"

"I know, that was their first mistake, sending so few."

Chapter 14

DETECTIVE DIRK SMITH checked into a casino near Silver Lake, just north of Pentwater, shortly after 6:00 pm. Detroit PD only allotted $75.00 per night for lodging, but Dirk kicked in an extra $50.00 so he could stay at a decent place. The casino qualified as that; besides, he was always happy to gamble.

He was currently seated in the small lounge just off the casino floor. It was an ultra-modern mix of chrome, red leather, neon lights, and glass. The electronic beeps and dings from the various slot machines were as ubiquitous as sirens in Detroit.

Dirk chose a small booth in the corner with his back to the wall. He took a generous sip of his third bourbon and gently rattled the ice in his glass. He was hoping to drown his disappointment in alcohol, but so far it wasn't working. He thought back to the day's events, which, in retrospect, were an epic failure. Not only did he not meet with the girl informant, but he was not able to speak with the deputy either. Why didn't the girl show up? He wondered. His best theory was that the whole thing was a setup, and both he, and the deputy, were supposed to be in the diner at the time of the attack.

The girl had probably summoned the deputy there as well. What he couldn't figure out was why was the gang worried about him. Dirk had zilch until the girl called him. No leads whatsoever. So why would they want to attack him? Did they think he knew something he didn't?

His working theory was that the girl was telling the truth when she initially called, and her brother somehow found out. He then decided to let Dirk come to the meeting and give him an example of what would happen to him if he didn't back off. That seemed plausible as well; after all, the girl sure sounded genuine on the phone.

One thing was for sure, Dirk thought: the gang was concerned about the deputy, and him, so they must be on the right track. He gulped the last of his bourbon and waved to the lone waitress. The plump gal, in a too-small black and white skirt and blouse, backtracked towards him, flashing him a fake smile. He ordered another Buffalo Trace over ice and a specialty burger as well.

Dirk wasn't about to be deterred so easily. He was onto something here. He felt it. He had spent the afternoon at the sheriff's department and was even allowed to sit in on the interviews of the cute owner of the diner and her cook. Something didn't add up with that guy, Dirk thought. He mysteriously appeared in town just yesterday, and today he disabled three guys, and scared off a fourth, from one of the most violent motorcycle gangs in the nation. Dirk and many other Detroit PD officers had plenty of dealings with the Devil's Dungeon over the years. They were stone-cold brutal killers. No one took them on single-handedly—at least, no one with a will to live.

Apparently, the local sheriff and his deputies were too busy congratulating the guy for saving their deputy's ass to have noticed how strange the circumstances were. The few questions they did ask about the cook's background was way too general. Dirk would do his own checking on the guy.

One thing was for sure: he wasn't just a cook that just happened to get lucky in a fight. The guy had serious skills and was in town for a reason besides grilling burgers. Dirk had a vast network of connections from various agencies, both state and federal. He would use them to find out who, and what, this cook really was.

Chapter 15

COLTON EXITED MAGGIE'S car and slowly walked to its rear. The seven bikers stopped several yards back and shut down the bikes. The sudden silence was almost as deafening as the seven loud exhausts had been.

"You must be the cook from the diner," said a large, heavily muscled biker sporting a four-inch neon green mohawk, "I'm Sack."

Colton noticed that he slipped gracefully from his bike, especially for such a big guy. "Zack?" asked Colton.

"No, not Zack—Sack. I played three years as an offensive lineman for Michigan State. I had the records for sacks my Junior year."

"Ah, hence the nickname. Well, I'm impressed," offered Colton.

"You should be. You hurt some friends of mine. I imagine you know what happens next," Sack retorted.

The remaining six bikers dismounted their iron horses and started fanning out in a line behind Sack.

"Why only three years?" asked Colton.

"Huh?" asked Sack.

"Three years with Michigan State. Why only three?"

"I got caught messing with the coach's daughter. She was only fifteen. Bitch told me she was eighteen. I lost my scholarship and did two years in the joint."

"Well, it's good to know the prison rehabilitation program is working so well. Now that you're such a model citizen," Colton countered.

"You're a real funny guy. You're 'bout to get your ass kicked real bad, and you're still joking," Sack replied.

"Listen, Sack, this isn't necessary. I don't want to hurt anymore people today. Please, you and your friends just leave now."

Sack let out a short laugh that sounded like a seal's bark. He then looked over both his shoulders at his friends and said, "Can you believe this guy?" There was nervous laughter from the other six.

"Tell you what, cook. I'm going to fight you solo. I don't need any help. When I stomp you good, and you're on the ground moaning with a few of your teeth missing, I'm gonna get me a piece of that hot bod in the car you were sucking lips with a few seconds ago. When I'm finished with her, I suspect the other guys will want a turn too. Now, talk is over."

"Just one more thing, Sack. When I get done disabling you, do I have your word we drive out of here without any more interference, or do I have to beat down everyone?"

Sack shook his head from side to side, "You sure are ballsy. That's a deal, Cook." Sack grinned, shrugging off his leather jacket and handing it back to another biker. He was clad in a black tank top. It was obvious he spent a lot of time pumping iron. His arms were huge, almost fake looking. A sure sign of frequent steroid usage. Matching tattoos of eagle talons covered each shoulder and barbed-wire tattoos encircled his biceps.

Sack did a few shoulder shrugs, rolled his head from side to side, then suddenly, without warning, lowered his head and charged like a bull.

Colton anticipated the charge but was still surprised at how fast Sack moved. Colton charged forward as well, knowing this was what Sack least expected. A guy his size was used to people running away from him, not at him. This unexpected action slowed Sack for a millisecond, as indecision and surprise flooded his mind by Colton's bold move. A millisecond was all the time Colton needed.

Sack was in a half-crouch, like he had been so many times before, charging the line, in an effort to tackle the quarterback. Colton, still in full stride, hurdled up and over Sack, and while directly above him kicked him hard in the nose. The sickening sound of crushing cartilage was louder than Sack's scream of pain. Colton landed on both feet directly behind him, nose to nose with the line of other bikers, who scrambled back in shock.

Sack was cupping his nose with his hands. Blood quickly poured into them from his shattered nose. Colton spun around and kicked hard at the back of Sack's knee. The knee caved inward, and Sack started to fall to his left. Colton stepped up quickly and placed him in a chokehold, keeping a vise-like lock on his neck. Sack thrashed about, but Colton held firm.

"Nappy time Sack sleep well. And remember, I'm a chef, not a cook."

Sack grunted one last time. His face flushed a bright red as he flailed about, but Colton continued to apply steady pressure to his neck. Finally, Sack went limp, like an over-cooked spaghetti noodle. Colton gently lowered him to the ground and looked expectantly at the remaining six bikers.

"You guys mind moving your bikes so I can get out of here?" Colton asked nonchalantly.

The remaining bikers exchanged glances with each other. They all remembered what happened to Skunk earlier that day.

As if reading their minds, Colton said, "Just tell your boss after I kicked Sack's ass that I ran for it."

"You can't take us all," said one member, Jimmy.

"Do you really believe that? I took out four of you this morning and didn't even break a sweat. Three of them are still in the hospital. You want to roll? Let's roll," Colton challenged.

The indecision was obvious on Jimmy's face. He glanced at the unmoving Sack and his nervous looking buddies before saying, "This ain't over, asshole."

"Is not over." Colton corrected him.

"What?" Jimmy asked.

"I said, is not over. Ain't is not a word. Seriously, how do you guys get through job interviews?" Colton asked.

"You won't be funny for long," Jimmy shot back. He nodded to the others, and they slowly pushed their bikes off the path.

Colton bent down and grabbed Sack under each arm, then dragged him off the path. "His leg should be fine after a few weeks on crutches; no broken bones, just torn tendons. His nose, well, that won't look so good. He should come around in a couple minutes."

Colton entered Maggie's car and started the engine. Maggie was smiling from ear to ear. "Who and what are you, Colton?" she asked. Colton turned to look out his rear window as he reversed down the two-track.

"I'm Colton. I'm a chef," He said, returning her smile as he backed out between the bikers.

Chapter 16

COLTON PULLED INTO the gravel driveway of Maggie's beachside bungalow. The sun appeared to be half-submerged into Lake Michigan. Colton almost expected to see giant steam clouds erupting all around it. The diffused, orange-red, glow reflected off the partial cumulus clouds above giving them a spectacular color. It was a near perfect, early October evening. The lake water was very still as though it was settling down for the evening.

"Incredible view," offered Colton.

"I know. I never get tired of it. Come on, quick before it's gone."

With that Maggie jumped from the car and ran toward the sandy beach. Colton chased after her. A nearby neighbor had a small fire burning. Swirls of grayish-white smoke drifted their way. Colton inhaled, enjoying the earthy wood smoke, mixed with the aromas of fresh lake water. A group of seagulls scattered as Maggie ran towards them, crying their displeasure as they half hopped, half flew, several yards away.

Maggie kicked off her flats and waded into the surf knee deep. Colton slipped from his shoes, quickly rolled up his jeans, and joined her.

"Isn't it beautiful?" She asked, as she slipped her arm around his waist resting her hand on his hip, while gazing at the sunset.

Her touch felt like an electric current running through him, despite the cool water, he was warm. He laid his arm across her shoulders. "It sure is."

"I'm worried, Colton. These bikers are serious. They will come after you again."

"I know, but I can handle them, don' t worry about me. Do they know you live here?"

"I don't think so. I've never seen them around here; besides, the deputies will be checking on me. It's you I'm concerned about. There are too many. I mean you were awesome today, unbelievable, but they won't quit. They will keep coming after you."

"Maggie. Please, don't worry about me. Don't forget about the sheriff department. They'll be watching those guys real close. Besides, I have a few friends I can call on if things get out of hand," Colton reassured her.

Maggie suddenly turned toward him. She wrapped her other arm around his waist. "You don't think things are out of hand now? These guys attacked Matt, and you twice, just today!" She said mildly exasperated.

Colton smiled, then replied, "Actually, I attacked them the first time. So, technically, they only attacked me once today. I've been in worse situations and came out on top. Trust me Maggie, I'll be fine."

"Stop talking and kiss me," Maggie said as she pulled herself closer to him.

Colton melted into her embrace. He kissed her tenderly. She kissed him back eagerly. After several seconds he pulled his lips away then rested his forehead against hers. The cool water lapped about their legs. Colton smiled.

"What?" inquired Maggie.

"You're absolutely beautiful," He replied.

"I bet you say that to all the girls," She teased.

"Only the beautiful ones."

"Well, thank you. You are kind of cute yourself," she said with a laugh.

Maggie suddenly turned toward her house and started walking that way, pulling him along while still clutching his hand. The sun now had settled below the horizon.

"I'm starving. I want to make you dinner, but first wine. You do drink wine don't you?" She asked.

"On occasion I allow myself to indulge," He replied with a grin.

Once inside Maggie poured each of them a generous amount of Chardonnay. Colton stood in her kitchen, leaning against a small counter with two stools. The interior was decorated beach-house style. Casual, comfortable furniture, subtle seafoam blues and yellows throughout. The living room had a fieldstone fireplace and wood flooring with a large oval rug.

"Nice place," he mused.

"Thanks. My parents originally purchased it as their summer weekend home. They were born and raised in Toledo."

"Toledo, Spain?"

"No silly. Toledo, Ohio. It's just a few hours south of here. Where are you from anyhow?"

"Oh no you don't, I want to hear about you," Colton protested.

Maggie took a sip of her wine while walking to a small couch. She sat down and patted the seat next to her. Colton sat beside her. The couch was small, and their thighs touched.

"What do you want to know?" Maggie asked.

"Anything and everything you want to tell me."

"Well. I'm an only child. I was born in Toledo. My mom and dad owned a small diner downtown and we came here to vacation every summer for a couple weeks. They fell in love with the area. When I was eight, they decided to buy the diner here in Pentwater, and everything was wonderful for five years until my Mom suddenly died of cancer. I was 13. My dad remarried the wicked witch of the west, a few years later. Thankfully, when I was twenty-two, he retired to Florida with the witch, and made me the majority owner of the diner."

"I'm sorry about your mother. That was way too young to die, and you were too young not to have a mom. Especially, since it sounds like your stepmother and you do not get along too well, " he offered.

"We have our differences that is for sure. Amber helped me through the tough times."

"The nurse at the hospital?"

"Yes, the shameless flirt."

Colton laughed.

"How about you?" She asked.

Colton didn't want to talk about his upbringing. He knew by not opening up to her, as she did to him, would not come across well, but he felt he had no choice. He didn't want to lie to her.

"I'm really sorry, Maggie, but can we talk about it some other time?"

Maggie hesitated before replying, "Ok, but please tell me you're not married, and you're not a criminal."

Colton laughed again before replying, "Neither of those; I can assure you."

Maggie wondered why he was so reticent but decided not to press the issue.

"I'm going to start dinner," Maggie said.

"That sounds great," Colton said, happy to be off the topic of his past. "Why don't you let me help?"

"Not a chance. I hope you like pan-fried Whitefish."

"I love pan-fried fish but can't say I ever had Whitefish."

"You will love it."

Maggie stood and grabbed the TV remote from the coffee table and clicked it on. She tossed the remote to Colton. "Make yourself comfortable. It'll be ready in 45 minutes," She then walked into the nearby kitchen.

The TV was on a 24-hour news channel. The anchorman had just announced that there was an attempt on the Pope's life, but details were sparse as it was breaking news. Colton bolted upright while turning the volume up. The anchorman confirmed what he said about an attempt on the pope's life and went to a live report from the Vatican.

The on-scene correspondent, a raven-haired Italian beauty that Colton had once dated, explained that details were very sketchy, but a reliable source advised the pope was attacked in his private chapel just before midnight. She continued that the attack was within the Vatican and occurred while the pontiff was alone saying his nightly prayers.

Apparently, the attacker was subdued and was currently in custody. She advised that the pope's condition was unknown, but an air ambulance arrived and departed the Vatican twenty minutes ago. The Vatican had yet to release an official statement.

Colton stood, and walked shakily to the kitchen. Here he was thousands of miles away, supposedly addressing a future threat to the pontiff, when someone, somehow attacked him at the Vatican.

Maggie was just dredging a fish fillet through beer batter and was immediately struck by Colton's ashen appearance.

"Is something wrong?" She asked.

"Yes, something is very wrong, but I can't get into it. I'm really sorry," With that said, Colton turned and walked out the front door without another word.

Maggie chased after him. "Colton, what is wrong. Please tell me!"

"I'm sorry, Maggie, I can't, not now. I don't know yet, um, please, I have to go. Can I borrow your car? I'll have it back in time for you to get to work. I promise."

"Let me drive you. Just let me turn off the stove first."

Maggie ran back into the house, turned off the burners, and quickly chugged the remainder of her glass of wine while wondering what the hell was going on.

Chapter 17

LUCAS WAS FURIOUS. "How in the hell did you let him get away?"

"Like I said boss, after he bested Sack, he jumped in the car and took off. When we tried to follow, two sheriff cruisers just happened to be driving by," Jimmy lied. The other five bikers who had been there nodded their heads in unison, not unlike a row of bobble-head dolls.

"Shit! who is this guy anyway? How in the hell can he take on my best guys? He takes out Marcus and Sack in the same day. Those two guys never lose a fight. I'll tell you one thing, no more bullshit, half-ass encounters with this punk. We are going to plan it out. Take him out on our terms, not his." Lucas hammered his fist down on the butcher block bar, so hard two empty beer bottles fell over.

"Good idea. We should probably lay low for a while as all the cops are going to be gunning for us anyhow," replied Jimmy. He was no dummy. He recalled what Lucas did to Skunk earlier in the day, and knew he had to stroke his ego to stay alive.

"Yeah, I know. We need to let the sheriff think we didn't know that Scotty was going to beat his deputy. We'll let him think that he acted on his own because he was drunk," agreed Lucas.

"But they're also going to want Skunk for holding a blade to that girl that owns the diner," replied Jimmy.

"Don't worry about that. I'll tell them he took off as he knew the heat was on him. We need to smooth this over quickly. I'm not ready to leave this area yet. It's making us way too much cash, especially with the college kids. They know how to party. We can barely keep up with their oxy and Adderall orders."

"Yeah, and it sure as hell beats cooking Meth. That shit is dangerous," said Jimmy, who should know, as his older brother (a previous member) blew himself up, and his trailer, into a million pieces a few years ago, after botching the mixture. His girlfriend at the time, Linda, was just pulling into the driveway and was spared any injury. Since then Linda earned the adjective, lucky, before her name.

Lucas walked behind the bar and yanked open the stainless-steel door of the cooler. He grabbed a bottle of Bud, twisted off the cap and drained half the bottle in one long pull.

"You are right about that Jimmy. You are not a dumbass like Skunk was, that is what I like about you. You have half a brain. Ok, here is how we play it. You and I are going to go recruit someone. Get Lucky Linda and tell her to put on that black outfit she wore last weekend at the pig roast. Tell her to look really hot, but to make sure she covers up her tattoos. I want her looking like a professional."

"Ok, but damn, it must be a special guy you got in mind, using Linda to entice him."

"It is. We are going to recruit us a deputy. I know just the one," offered Lucas with a grin.

"A deputy! Are you sure that's a good idea?"

Jimmy was feeling good, now that Lucas told him he had half a brain. He was just stupid enough to think that was a compliment.

"It's a great idea, not a good idea. Cops are people just like everyone else. They have desires and needs. I've seen a guy at the Riverbend Tavern every time I've delivered there. I asked the owner about him. He told me he is there almost every night. He is a deputy that is seriously pissed off that he never got promoted. He's still a road deputy after 27 years. He's been divorced four times and isn't married now. Best of all he owes almost his whole paycheck to support a half-dozen kids. He's ripe for the picking. We are going to get us inside access to the sheriff department."

Lucas drained the other half of the bottle before belching long and loud. "Now, go get the bitch and be back here in a half hour."

Lucas grabbed a fresh Budweiser and wondered again where Allison had gone off to. No one had seen her all day, but he didn't have time to worry about her now. He wandered into his office and shut the door, then fired up a bowl of Blue Dream that arrived from Colorado just the day before. He inhaled deeply while sitting down at his desk. He felt the change come over him, not from the drug, but from Botis.

Botis first came to him in a dream about a year ago. The incredibly vivid dreams were not like any he ever had before. They continued for a month straight. Botis revealed who he was and what he needed from Lucas. He would wake up thinking he was going crazy. He even quit all drugs and alcohol for two weeks but still dreamed of Botis nightly.

After a month or so, Lucas realized he didn't even need to be sleeping for Botis to appear to him, or rather, inhabit his mind. He didn't really care as he agreed with Botis on most things. The most important thing was that Botis despised the same individual he did and even had a plan to eliminate him. Lucas took another hit of Blue Dream holding the smoke in his lungs as long as possible before slowly exhaling. He smiled at the relaxation seeping into every nerve of his being as Botis was doing the same.

He booted up his Dell computer and typed out another letter to the single individual he loathed more than anyone in the world. He told the weak, old man once again how he despised him and the institution he represented. He kept it short and smiled to himself at his last paragraph. Threats were part of all of his letters, but he stepped it up a notch this time letting the Shepherd of the stupid lambs know he had less than a month to live.

Lucas donned a set of surgical gloves and printed the letter. He then meticulously sketched the tiny figure on the bottom corner of the letter prior to sealing it in an envelope. He would have Lucky Linda mail it later in the week from Wisconsin. He had her take a weekly ferry across Lake Michigan to peddle some product in Milwaukee. No one would be tracing him from where he mailed the letter from, nor would they get any fingerprints or DNA, as he took precautions.

Lucas then switched over to Google. After a few seconds of searching, he confirmed the Pope's visit to the Michigan Minor Basilica near Detroit was still on.

In three weeks, the supreme Catholic sheepherder would be visiting the great state of Michigan. Lucas would be there to welcome him along with Botis. Lucas would show the weak old man that it was a mistake to come to his state.

Chapter 18

ALLISON KNOCKED HESITANTLY on the side door of the rectory. A single yellow bulb was burning overhead casting a small halo of light in the otherwise full black night. After several seconds, she saw the curtain pull back an inch from the door's window. Father Carlos cautiously opened the door a few inches. "Allison, what are you doing here after dark?"

"I'm sorry, Father, but I'm really scared, there are a lot of things I need to tell you. I can't go back to my brother, not ever."

The priest opened the door and stood to the side. Allison entered the small foyer. "Let me wake Sister Rebecca." Father Carlos was none too comfortable being alone with Allison. She had been a frequent visitor the past couple months and had confessed to witnessing many sins that a girl of her age should not be exposed to, no doubt a product of her environment, but still, he must be cautious.

"Please don't wake her, Father, besides all of this can wait until morning," pleaded Allison.

"Allison, you simply can't spend the night here. Let me call Child Protective Services."

"No! They're useless. They never did anything to help me in Detroit. I need to talk to the police. I was supposed to meet with a detective from Detroit this morning, at the diner, but I chickened out."

"Let me call him now for you."

"Please, Father, I want to wait until morning. I'm exhausted. I had a really bad day. I'll let you call him in the morning, and I'll tell him everything. I promise."

"But your brother will be worried. He will be looking for you," protested the priest.

"He has worse problems than me right now. Please Father, I can't ever go back to him. He is very evil, more than you can imagine."

Father Carlos sighed. "Ok, but just for tonight. Use the guest room across from the kitchen. Help yourself to what you need from the pantry and fridge if you're hungry. Good night, my child." Father Carlos made the sign of the cross over her and whispered a prayer of protection for her.

Allison wandered into the attached church through a connecting door. The interior was very dark except for very dim lighting near the altar.

St. Michael's Church was much smaller than St. Gabriel, her Detroit Parish, but both had the same feeling of comfort. It had far fewer statues and religious art than St. Gabriel, but its crucifix that hung behind the altar captivated her. The life-size figure of Jesus was eerily real in its detail. The emotion edged in Christ's face captured the sadness that he must have felt at that moment like none other she had ever seen. She had read that the crucifix was imported from Rome, and once adorned an altar in that historic city.

Allison knelt in the first pew and made the sign of the cross. She bowed her head and thought back to earlier in the day when she ran into the woods fully intending to end her life.

Just prior to jumping from the limb, a lone bird descended from the sky and landed on a branch of an adjacent tree only a few feet away. Allison was startled to see it was a mourning dove. It looked curiously at her. She knew her bible and knew that a dove was indeed a biblical bird. She was immediately filled with a sense of peace and forgiveness. The dove suddenly flew away.

Allison was certain this was a sign. She would tell the police all she knew. That is what the angel in her vision had told her to do before, but she had failed to do it. Feeling full of shame, she quickly untied the cord from her neck and climbed down to the ground. She knew what she had to do and would not live in fear of her brother any longer.

After several minutes of prayer, she went into the kitchen suddenly realizing she was famished. She made two ham and cheese sandwiches, found a bag of chips, and a can of pop, and devoured all within minutes. She tiptoed into the guest room and curled up on the bed and fell fast asleep.

Chapter 19

MAGGIE DROVE COLTON to his downtown apartment, mostly in silence. She stopped her car in front of his building not knowing what to say. Colton leaned across and kissed her on the cheek. "I'm sorry, it was nothing you did. I just can't get into it now."

"Ok. Will I see you tomorrow—at work?"

"Maggie, I'm not sure. I'm sorry. I'll try to be there, that's the best I can offer now."

He quickly kissed her on the cheek and jumped out of the car, then ran up the stairs to his room. He rushed inside and went directly to his closet where he removed a section of wood trim along the floorboard with his pocket knife. Inserting the knife blade between two panels of the planked wood flooring, he pried up a panel that exposed a small, black, leather attaché case.

Colton retrieved the case and carried it to his dining table where he manipulated the two rolling combination locks and opened the lid. A Sig-Sauer, Combat P220, .45 caliber pistol rested inside, snugged between foam rubber, along with a suppressor, two extended 10-round magazines full of ammunition, a cellular phone, two sets of false IDs, and passports.

Colton removed the phone and powered it up. This was no ordinary phone, but a secure satellite phone that operated on an encrypted frequency that even the esteemed NSA couldn't intercept. Colton punched in a 12-digit number from memory. A man's voice answered with a coded greeting in German. Colton authenticated who he was. There was a brief pause before the Controller answered in Italian.

"Is he alive?" Colton asked without preamble in his native Italian.

"Yes, actually he is fine, besides a few bruises," answered his controller.

"Thank God."

"And thank Michael; it was he that saved Papa."

"Tell me everything," Colton implored.

"Michael had turned in early but claimed he had a dream that summoned him to Papa's chapel. He wasn't a second too early. The lone Swiss Guard outside the chapel had heard nothing, but Papa was but a few seconds away from most certainly being beaten badly, even killed."

"Claimed to have a dream. Come now, you still doubt, after all you have seen and heard the past few years," Colton rebuked his boss, "What was the motive?"

"A member of the janitorial staff had secreted himself inside the chapel prior to Papa's arrival. He threatened him with a large wrench. Botis does not appear to have been involved. Preliminary interrogation revealed that the janitor is a member of an ultra-conservative movement that is upset with Papa's direction on many issues."

"And, regarding the alleged dream of Michael's, we haven't time for this debate again," the controller replied, finishing with a deep sigh. "Don't worry, all is in control here, although, I suspect some heads will roll with the Swiss guard in the morning. His Eminence will see to that. Luckily, the guard are not my concern. What progress have you made? I've been expecting a call prior to now."

"I'm in Pentwater and have made a couple contacts with the gang, but not the target. A meeting will be coming soon," Colton replied.

"You are keeping things discreet, I trust. Not drawing attention to yourself, I hope, and not getting distracted?"

I had to handle a couple situations, but you won't see them on the national news—all survived," Colton replied, knowing full well what the Controller meant by distracted. He wasn't about to mention Maggie, because she was not a distraction. He lied to himself.

"Very well, stay on task and get things done. I don't think this incident will affect Papa's travel plans. We need to be sure if Botis is actually in play that he is taken out well before then."

"I'm on task. Tell Michael I said good work." Colton then severed the connection and returned the phone to the case. He carried the case back to the floor carefully covering it back up with the floor planks.

Colton walked to his mini refrigerator and selected a bottle of Heineken. He found a bottle opener and popped the top. He let the bottle breath for a minute while thinking how much he missed his hometown brew pubs, or micro-breweries, as they were fond of calling them here in the States. Micro-breweries were nothing new in Rome; monks had been brewing small batches of craft brews there for hundreds of years. Wine wasn't the only alcoholic beverage Italy was famous for.

Recalling his phone conversation with the controller Colton sighed. *What a misnomer that is,* Colton thought to himself; everyone that knew Colton knew all too well that no one could control him. Colton took a long pull of the cold beer. He moved the bottle from his lips and placed it against his forehead to help with the start of a headache. It was time to get busy.

He had hoped, especially with a romance blooming, to take some more time here—a week or two. Heal some emotional, and mental scars, before creating new ones. He liked Maggie a lot, but it was probably best this way. He would only be using her to assuage his own wounds and needs. That was selfish. He did sense that she needed some healing herself, but how could he help her? In the long run, he would only hurt her more. His career choice was not conducive to a steady relationship, quite the opposite.

He sighed again in frustration and realized that now he was being selfish. Maybe he was getting too distracted—again. The pontiff had survived a close call tonight. He didn't need another one in a few weeks.

It was time to get proactive. It was time to stop reacting to their moves. He took another swig of beer before returning the bottle to his forehead. Tomorrow he would make certain he met Lucas Sledge, even if he had to walk in the clubhouse front door.

Chapter 20

LINDA KORNER, A.K.A, "Lucky Linda," strutted into the Riverbend Saloon at a little past 9:00 pm. The place was only a third full. It was a little too late for the dinner crowd, and a little too early for the bar crowd. Nevertheless, Jeff Nowak was in his usual stool at the far end of the bar, closest to the elevated television, nursing a low-end scotch.

Jeff was bitter. He worked diligently for the sheriff's department for over 27 years and had little to show for it. He was still a road deputy, and an average one at that. He had taken his share of promotional exams, but never fared too well. Half the force was half his age but acted like they owned the place. The new breed was everything he wasn't— smart, athletic, health conscious, and worst of all, several were already sergeants.

Jeff was only three years from retirement but had little to no savings. Three divorces and four kids later, the dual-edged sword of alimony and child support cut deeply. He needed a woman to take care of him, but the years had not aged well on him.

He wasn't fat, he was soft. He wasn't tall, but he wasn't short either. He wasn't handsome, but you wouldn't call him ugly. At 48 years of age, most women paid him little, if any attention.

Jeff was contemplating all the cruelties the world had inflicted upon him when Linda caught his eye. He saw her in the bar mirror. She entered the place like she owned it. She strutted over to a barstool, wearing six-inch black stilettos, like she was working a fashion runway in Paris.

Jeff liked what he saw. Linda was wearing a white, short-sleeved, satin blouse, unbuttoned enough to reveal more than ample, albeit, artificial breasts. Her blouse was tucked into a short, tight, black leather skirt with an oversized black belt. Her bleached, blond hair was short and spiky on top. but longer in the back. Her 5'5" frame carried her 125 pounds nicely, and her outfit accentuated her tan legs. At thirty-five. despite a hard life, Linda still looked to be in her late twenties.

Linda smiled briefly at Jeff while hiking herself up on a barstool, two down from him, purposely letting her short skirt ride up even higher, and not bothering to smooth it down. Jeff quickly forgot all about his problems and discreetly took sideways glances at her legs.

Jeff was certain she was new to town. He knew most everyone. He was starting to feel better about life while imagining himself with her. She met his gaze and smiled shyly at him, but the moment was broken by the approaching barmaid. Linda ordered a gin & tonic. The barmaid then asked Jeff if he was good. Jeff was about to reorder his usual cheap scotch, but the liquid courage of three prior scotches fueled his reply. "No, I'll have a Johnnie Walker Black, on the rocks, and put the beautiful, young lady's drink on my tab."

The barmaid smiled to herself thinking, *don't even try it Jeff she is way out of your league,* but said, "sure thing," instead, and busied herself with the order.

"Thank you. It isn't often anymore that you run into a real gentleman. I'm Linda."

"I'm sorry to hear that, because if anyone treats you less than kindly, they should be arrested," Jeff said in reply. He knew some women liked cops, and he would play that card early, hoping to give him a better chance.

"You talk like a police officer. You wouldn't be one by chance, would you? I've always admired policemen," she said in a soft, sweet voice while turning toward him. The movement hiked the skirt up another inch.

Jeff's pulse quickened. *Holy crap,* he thought, *this chick is hitting on me!* "Actually I am. I'm Jeff, and it's very nice to meet you, "he replied.

"Very nice to meet you too Jeff," she said, then slid off the stool and sat next to him. He now stared at her ample breasts that were straining the fabric of her thin blouse.

"How do they look?" she asked.

Jeff knew he was caught looking, and figured he probably blew any chance he had, but then he felt her hand rest on his upper thigh.

The barmaid returned and set their drinks down. "Thanks, Stacey, just add them to my tab," Jeff said barely taking his eyes off Linda.

"Sure thing," Stacey said and walked back to the other end of the bar thinking to herself, *Well, what the hell, must be a high-end hooker in town,* after noticing the woman and Jeff's fast connection.

Linda left her hand on his thigh and asked in a soft, seductive voice, "Do you have a gun?" while dragging the tip of her tongue across her pink upper lip.

John felt his temperature rising and his breathing became faster.

"Sure, I mean, of course," he stammered.

"Would you let me hold it sometime?"

"Hell, yes I will. You can even shoot it if you want," he answered.

She left her hand in place on his thigh, while picking up her drink with her other hand. "I would like that a lot. I just arrived here yesterday. I'm a writer and thought this would be a great place to start research for my new book," She replied then sipped her drink.

"That is really interesting. What are you writing?"

She smiled coyly, "I'm a therapist. I write self-help books. I encourage people to be creative and live life to their fullest."

"That sounds like a book I would love to read. What kind of therapist are you?"

"A sex therapist, and if you want, you can help me with my research while I'm here." She said this in a soft, husky tone while leaning towards him and sliding her hand higher up his thigh.

"Stacey, I need my bill, honey," Jeff yelled a bit too loud.

Many hours later, Lucky Linda dressed silently in the dark bedroom. Deputy Nowak snored loudly nearby. Linda figured he would sleep most of the day. She had kept him very busy most of the night. He was all hers, which meant all theirs. Lucas would be very happy.

She scribbled out a quick note for Jeff leaving it on his kitchen table, along with her cellphone number. She lied that he was the best she ever had. He wasn't the worst, as part of the life of being an associate female member of the Devil's Dungeon was that she was community property during her probation. That was the longest six months of her life.

She slipped quietly out the side door of the old cottage. It was one of five that were set up near the river. They were primarily rented out as fishing cabins. The property owner lived in Arizona and utilized the deputy as a live-in manager, custodian, and maintenance man, in exchange for a free place to live. Jeff told Linda all this last night during their brief rest periods.

A few early rising fishermen were loading up their SUV's with thier equipment and gave Linda inquiring stares.

"Morning boys," she said, "anyone heading towards town? I could use a lift."

She was riding in the front seat of a Chevy Tahoe a couple minutes later heading into town. The sun was just coming up, the inky black sky was turning indigo. She was more than halfway back to the lodge when she reached the old Catholic Church. She gazed up at the tall steeple with the big, white cross illuminated on top.

    Linda's gaze was interrupted by movement near the front of the church. She saw a girl walking up the church stairs carrying the morning newspaper. It was Allison, no doubt about it. She must have been out all night. Lucas wouldn't be very happy to hear this news. She would wake him as soon as she got back.

Chapter 21

FATHER CARLOS WAS SURPRISED to see Allison in the kitchen eating cereal and reading the paper she had already retrieved from outside. He kissed her lightly on the forehead. "Good morning, my child. You certainly are up early."

"Morning, father. Sister Rebecca told me to remind you that she had to be at the beach for the sunrise prayer circle but would be back by nine."

"Oh. Yes, I did forget she was leading that this week. Well, I see you have your breakfast. I will be with you in a few minutes as I have to unlock the church and say my morning prayers; afterwards, we will talk."

Father Carlos unlocked the entrance doors to the church and gazed out at the brightening dawn. It was just light enough to see storm clouds far off to the west. He returned to the front of the church and was kneeling before the altar reciting the rosary, when he heard someone enter the rear doors. Glancing over his shoulder, he observed the mysterious man from a few days ago hesitantly approach.

"Good morning," offered the priest. He stood clutching an ivory rosary with a rose-colored crucifix.

"Good morning, father; I'm sorry to interrupt," Colton replied.

"No problem, but we don't have a mass on Saturday mornings, just the evening mass at 6 o'clock."

"I know. I just want to pray a bit, if that's ok."

"Absolutely. Take all the time you need. Is everything ok?"

"I hope so, father, but I am deeply concerned about our pontiff."

"Ahhh—yes, that was a bit of a shock, but CNN is advising he didn't suffer any serious wounds. He will get through this, but certainly it is a time for prayer."

"It may be time for more than that father."

The kindly priest looked at Colton with an inquiring stare. He was not certain whom this man was, but despite his odd confessions a few days prior, he trusted him.

"You speak as though you suspect our Holy Father is still in danger. The national news indicates the man responsible was apprehended."

"The American news outlets seem to be master storytellers, as opposed to unbiased reporters of fact, father, but yes, the suspect was apprehended and no longer poses a threat. However, the Holy Father will always be a target."

Father Carlos now struggled how to say what needed to be said. He knew from this man's confession that he was capable of extreme violence, and in fact, if he spoke the truth, seemed to be plagued by it.

"You suggest that it may be time for more than prayer. Forgive me for saying this, but from your confession you seem to be a man of considerable violent action. Confessions are confidential, of course, but if I feel there is a threat towards the pope—"

"Then, you must notify your bishop, who will notify his cardinal, who will place a call to Rome, and be connected with the head of the Vatican Swiss Guard, who will assign it a case number and will have someone further investigate it to determine its credibility," finished Colton.

Father Carlos stared at Colton for several seconds before responding in a near whisper. "Who exactly are you?"

"I'm a chef."

"You appear well versed in security procedures for threats against the Holy Father for a simple chef."

"I consider myself more of a complex chef," Colton replied, a slow grin spreading across his face.

Father Carlos returned the smile. "I feel that you are not a threat at all . . . at least not to the pontiff or his Holy Church. And you speak of the American news as though you are not an American. Surprisingly, I do not detect an accent but if I had to hazard a guess, I would say you are Italian."

"Father, I am not a threat to the pope, or the Holy Church, quite the opposite." Ignoring the American comment Colton rapidly changed gears, feeling he had already divulged too much. He asked, "Do you know about the leader of the Devil's Dungeon here in town?"

"I do, indeed, know of this individual," Father Carlos replied hesitantly.

"He is a very dangerous man, father. You must be very careful around him. If he ever comes here call 911 immediately. I also have reason to believe his little sister may have reached out to you. If she has, I cannot tell you enough how much danger you may be in."

Colton was a master of reading facial clues, and body language in general.

"What is it, father?"

"She is in my rectory now," the visibly paling priest replied.

There was a creaking of a door from the far side of the church. A young teenage girl walked tentatively inside. Both men turned to look at her. She looked startled at first, then broke into a big toothy grin.

"I knew you would come for me," she said while gazing at Colton.

She walked towards him trying unsuccessfully to hold back tears that cascaded down her cheeks. "I dreamed of you again last night. You look the same, except for your clothes." She frowned at his blue jeans and worn leather jacket. "You wore a shining white robe with a red sash. Father meet my guardian angel," Allison said.

Colton laughed a soft, quiet laugh. "Sorry to disappoint you, but I'm hardly an angel. You must be Allison."

The quiet morning dawn was shattered by two loud Harleys pulling up out front. Allison and Father Carlos both exchanged panicked glances.

"Do exactly as I say," Colton said.

Less than a minute later, Lucas stormed into the church with his sergeant in arms, Sumo, in tow. "Allison. I know you're here!" His booming voice filled with rage was incongruous with the calm, incensed-infused, candlelit interior of the old church.

"Please quiet down; I am in the middle of a confession," said Father Carlos from a nearby confessional.

Lucas stalked through a row of pews toward the confessional. "I know who you have in that booth, preacher man."

"I'm afraid that whoever is in the confessional is of no concern to you. Now, please sit down, and I will be with you in a few minutes," Father Carlos calmly replied from inside the confessional.

Lucas stormed over to the confessional door marked penitent, opposite the priest's door, and yanked it open. He was surprised to see a man wearing jeans, a t-shirt, and a well-worn, brown, leather jacket with long dark hair and serious eyes. "Who in the hell are you, and where is Allison?"

Colton slowly stood from the tiny red velvet stool and met the furious gaze of Lucas. "Let me guess—you're the infamous Lucas Sledge. I'm Colton, the guy that put four of your followers in the hospital. I would say "nice to meet you," but I'm in church, and I don't want to lie. Now, if you don't mind, please step out of my way. I get a bit claustrophobic."

Lucas remained where he was, blocking Colton's egress from the small booth. He sized up Colton. He could tell the man was not afraid of him as most people were.

"I thought you would be bigger," Lucas finally said.

"I get that a lot, but size isn't everything, as you should know."

"Just like my guys said, a real smart ass."

"I'm surprised your guys can talk. They didn't have much to say after I was through with them. Actually, I'm glad you came by; I was planning on stopping by your place later today."

"Really, well, that would have been interesting."

"I'm sure it would have been. Now, step away from the door," ordered Colton.

Lucas clenched both his fists. "Why don't you make me."

Colton inhaled deeply then let out his breath slowly. "I would much rather you step aside. Father Carlos is probably getting tired of hearing my confessions. I would hate to have him sit down with me again in such a short time."

Father Carlos now exited the adjoining confessional holding a cell phone. "Please leave. The police are on their way. I do not want any trouble. What is it you want?"

Lucas would never admit it to anyone, but he was a bit unnerved about the confidence of the smart-mouth chef, especially coupled with the fact that he had already easily beat some of his best men. He turned to the priest and said, "I don't want any trouble either just tell me where my sister is."

The priest remained silent.

"Remaining silent is not an option, padre. Another priest tried to keep my sister from me before. Things didn't end up so well for him. I was hoping you were smarter."

"Is that a confession?" asked Colton.

"What. You a cop, besides a cook?"

"I don't know, Botis, you tell me. Am I?"

Lucas was stunned. He wasn't sure he heard the cook correctly. "What the hell did you call me?"

"You heard me right, Botis, and Hell is where you belong. Now move out of my way!" Colton shouted and shoved Lucas with both hands. Lucas toppled off his feet falling on the floor between the pews, while Colton stepped out of the confessional.

Lucas' partner, aptly named Sumo due to his extreme obesity, started towards Colton.

"No" yelled Lucas who struggled up, "He's mine."

"Bad decision, Lucas. I'm really curious how a guy like you got to be a leader making such bad decisions. Botis can't help you in here. You're on your own, just like you were when you killed that priest in Detroit, but no, I'm not a priest, nor am I Amish, so bring it on."

"You don't know what you're talking about. I didn't kill any priest, but I'm about to kill me a cook."

"Actually, I'm a chef."

Both of the church doors (front & side) suddenly swung open. Two deputies quickly entered each. The first two through had shotguns at the ready, the other two, handguns. "Morning father," said the oldest of the four. Colton recognized him as the same senior deputy from the diner and hospital. "Is there a problem here?"

Father Carlos glanced at Lucas and his obese companion. "No, we were all having a discussion. I believe Mr. Sledge, and his friend, were just leaving—correct, Mr. Sledge?"

Lucas turned towards the deputies. "That's correct, officers." He turned back to face Colton and whispered, "another time very soon."

"You can count on it," Colton answered.

Lucas glared at Colton, then turned away and walked towards the exit with Sumo following. The deputies stepped aside to allow them through. Lucas looked at the older deputy as he passed him. He stopped and read his nameplate, Deputy Lormar, and remarked, "kind of heavy firepower for a couple guys isn't it? Oh, by the way, how's Deputy Toney doing? Did he sleep good?"

Deputy Lormar holstered his handgun, then looked down at the floor and began nodding his head and mumbling something.

"What did you say?" asked Lucas as he stopped and faced the older cop. The other two deputies walked towards them. Deputy Lormar lifted his hand in a stop gesture to them, then lifted his head and looked directly at Lucas.

"I said thirty-eight more days. That is when I retire, and I won't have to deal with pieces of crap like you anymore. If you are trying to get me to do something stupid give it up. By the way. do you have any spares?"

"Any what?"

"Any spares," repeated the deputy.

"Spare what?"

"Spare tires. Kind of odd how both your bikes have flat tires front and back, don't ya think? You guys must have driven over some nails or glass." The silver-haired deputy flashed a slow smile.

Lucas stormed out of the church followed closely by all four deputies. Indeed, all four tires were flat on their Harleys. He spun back towards the deputies, "you sons of bitches!"

Deputy Lormar casually strode towards him and stopped a foot away. "You accusing us of this? They were like that when we pulled up."

"Bullshit!" hollered Lucas.

"I suggest you get on your bikes and ride them back to your clubhouse before I call a wrecker and have them impounded. By the way, Deputy Toney slept very well, but your probationary bitch, that sucker-punched him, seems to have slipped in the jail shower. He has a couple bad shiners. Looks like a racoon," Lormar said as he rubbed his raw knuckles of his right hand.

Lucas stared at the deputy for a moment then mounted his bike.

Sumo started to protest, "We'll screw up the rims, if we ride 'em like this."

"Shut the fuck up and get on your bike and ride," ordered Lucas. The two drove slowly onto the street, their tires making flap-flap-flap noises as they rode unsteadily away.

Once they were out of sight, Colton talked Allison into going with the deputies. Deputy Lormar assured him that he would personally escort her to a foster family in another county. He would have the Detroit detective meet her there later today. Colton promised he would visit her in a few days.

She hugged him tightly. "If you have to kill him, I understand. I mean he is my brother, and I shouldn't say that, but it is what it is. Is that wrong?" she asked.

"Your feelings are your feelings, and you don't have to apologize for them.

I don't want to kill him and pray it doesn't come to that," Colton said.

He walked her to the patrol car. Deputy Lormar opened the door for her. Once she was in, he gently shut the door and walked Colton to the rear of the car.

"You need to be careful. I understand you had another run-in with the gang last night."

"How did you know that?" Colton asked.

"Another gang member comes into the hospital with a screwed-up knee and busted up nose. I'm not stupid. You may as well have autographed the wounds."

Colton shrugged. "It was self-defense."

"I'm not complaining. I'm your biggest fan—but be careful."

"Can I ask you something?"

"Anything?"

"Do you know why Toney split with Maggie?"

Deputy Lormar nodded his head. "A deputy told me he saw Maggie drop you off at your apartment last night."

"Wow, information travels fast here."

"Small town," Lormar said, "Anyhow Maggie is good stuff. Great kid. I'm only telling you this cause of what you did for Toney. This stays between us—understood?"

"Yes sir"

"Toney broke it off because he suffers from Post-Traumatic Stress from his time in the Iraq desert. He never shared that with Maggie. He is dealing with it, but still has some serious bouts of depression. He didn't think Maggie deserved that. At least not until he knew he had it under control. He still loves her. He's a great guy."

"He should tell her. She thinks it is something she did wrong. I can tell she still loves him too," Colton offered.

"Not our decision; it's Toney's Hopefully, he gets his head right before she moves on. Maybe it's too late already," Lormar said while looking expectantly at Colton.

"No sir. Nothing has happened between us. Besides, I won't be in town much longer," Colton offered.

"You got somewhere else to be? You just started work here three days ago."

Colton sighed. "I had hoped to stay a bit longer, but truth is, I wasn't long for this town either way. I do have somewhere else I need to be."

"Well, say goodbye before you go," Lormar added. He shook Colton's hand, then entered his cruiser. As it pulled away, Allison leaned out the window and waved. Colton waved back then walked over to Father Carlos.

"Father, you need to be very careful. Lucas may still think you're hiding her. I have good reason to believe he was responsible for the murder of a priest near Detroit just a few months back," warned Colton.

"I know who Botis is. You called him that—why?" asked Father Carlos.

"Hell on Earth, father, Hell on Earth."

Father Carlos nodded his head in understanding. "Be careful, Be very careful."

"People keep telling me that."

"Looks like a storm is coming," Father Carlos remarked, as he gazed upward at a line of dark clouds rapidly approaching.

"It's already here, father," Colton said and walked away.

Chapter 22

MAGGIE FROWNED AS SHE unlocked the diner's front door. What had she said, or did, that made Colton leave so quickly last night, just when she thought all was going so well? She knew she was falling hard for him. Why wouldn't she? He was handsome, in great shape, made her laugh, and saved her life. What wasn't to like, she thought. After all, Matt wasn't interested in her anymore.

Truth was she knew very little about Colton. Something she hoped to remedy soon. If he hadn't already left town. She felt nauseated at just the mere thought of that.

A lone sheriff Crown Vic pulled into the lot. Deputy Jeff Nowak hopped out and practically skipped to the door. Maggie held it open for him. "Good morning, Jeff; you seem to be in an awfully good mood this morning."

"Morning to you Maggie," replied the usually gruff deputy.

He sauntered over to the counter and hopped onto a stool. Maggie poured him a tall cup of black coffee.

"Quiet shift so far?" asked Maggie.

"You would think so, on a Sunday morning and all, but a couple of damn bikers were causing problems at St. Michaels," the deputy answered.

"Seriously? What is their problem? I can't believe they're causing trouble at a church. I don't understand why you can't arrest the whole bunch."

"It's not that easy. Unfortunately, they have rights like everyone else. But we are keeping a close eye on them. In fact, your new cook, the town hero, was at the church too."

"Colton? What was he doing there?" Maggie asked with concern.

"I don't know. I was a little late on shift this morning, but from talking with the guys on scene, I think he was there talking with the priest about something."

"Anyhow, we sent a not so subtle message to the bikers; they mysteriously had their tires flattened while inside the church," Jeff answered, then took a sip of coffee.

"Good to hear. You want the usual?" Maggie inquired.

"Nope. Need to shape up a bit. How about some oatmeal?"

"Ok, what gives? You have had biscuits and gravy every Saturday morning for the past two years. Oatmeal—seriously?"

"Well, if you must know I met a lady friend. Don't get upset, I certainly asked you out enough." Jeff teased. "Anyhow, this one is a keeper for sure," smiled the deputy.

"You don't say. Well good for you Jeff. Is she from around here?"

"Nope. Just in town for a visit, but I have a good feeling about her."

"What does she do for a living?" Asked Maggie as she walked into the kitchen to prepare his order. She then peeked out the cook's window and said, "I can hear ya just fine. My cook's late—so I'm cooking."

"She's a sex therapist."

"Oh, wow, um that's different," Maggie stammered.

"It sure is, and I certainly learned you are never too old to learn new—"

"I get the point, Jeff. Please don't elaborate," pleaded Maggie.

Jeff laughed good naturedly. "Sorry, but she sure is something."

"How is Matt doing?" Maggie asked hoping to change the topic.

"He is doing well. It sounds as though he will be released in a couple days."

"That's good to hear."

"Look Maggie, it's not just me, but most of the guys at the station wonder why you haven't hooked up with someone else yet. I mean you're a beautiful gal, and it seems all you do is work. Life is too short for that."

"Thanks Jeff, but I doubt I should take relationship advice from you. Haven't you been divorced three times?"

"Ouch. You are not pulling any punches today. Be careful, I might not leave you much of a tip."

"If you leave me any less than usual, I'll have to start only giving you half cups of coffee."

The trio of tiny silver bells dangling from the entrance door jingled. Jeff and Maggie both looked that way. Colton walked in and nodded at the deputy, then pushed his way through the swinging doors into the kitchen.

"Good morning," Colton said to Maggie.

Maggie smiled and asked, "What are you doing here. You're not scheduled until noon. By the way, I heard you had an incident at the church. Everything ok?"

By the way she asked, Colton knew she was referring to much more that what had occurred at the church.

Colton sighed heavily, "We need to talk Maggie. I'm very sorry but I can't work here anymore. Something very important needs my full attention. I shouldn't have taken this job. I apologize, but please, I need to talk with you about this. Are your free tonight?"

Maggie studied his face for a long time not answering. She didn't like what she saw. She knew a break-up look when she saw it, but wasn't sure she could call it that, as they hadn't even dated yet. Still, she willed herself not to cry. What had she done wrong this time?

As though reading her mind Colton said, "Please, I'll try to explain everything. It wasn't anything you did." His tone was soft and apologetic.

"Sure, why don't you come over about six," She said tersely while walking out of the kitchen with Jeff's oatmeal before he could answer. She set the bowl down in front of Jeff and wiped a single tear from the corner of her eye before continuing towards the restroom in the rear of the restaurant.

Jeff had heard murmuring from the kitchen. It didn't take over twenty years of investigative experience to know that the two were an item or had been.

Colton pushed through the door and nodded again at Jeff.

"Morning," Jeff said. Then with a quieter voice remarked, "Whatever you do don't break her heart. She has had too much of that in her life, besides you would be a fool to do that. She's a great girl, and most guys in town would love to have her."

"I'm trying to avoid that, believe me I am. Tell Deputy Toney he'd be a fool to shut her out of his life," Colton said then walked out of the diner and whispered to himself, "dear Lord give me strength."

Chapter 23

DETECTIVE DIRK SMITH woke up with a pounding headache and a throat as dry as sandpaper. This was nothing new, as an alcoholic for over twenty years, he was prepared for it. He prided himself in never drinking while on the job, but the off hours were a different story.

He padded to the hotel bathroom in his undershorts, where he uncapped a bottle of ibuprofen and shook out three caplets into his mouth. He struggled a few seconds with the plastic wrapping that encased the plastic cup before filling it with water and swallowed the pills. He refilled the cup twice more and chugged each one down, in a futile effort to drown the dryness in his throat.

His cell phone chirped twice, at the bed nightstand, indicating he had just received a text. He retrieved his iPhone and was surprised to see it was already 9:30 in the morning. He struggled trying to conjure up a memory of what time he went to bed but couldn't. His last memory was of losing a couple hundred bucks at the blackjack table.

Scrolling through the text he now verified exactly what he suspected. The cook was not just a cook. While at the police station during his interview yesterday, Dirk had handed Colton a photo of Lucas Sledge, asking him if he was the gang member that had held Maggie at knifepoint. Colton assured him it wasn't, but Dirk didn't care about that.

After Colton had left, Dirk later packaged the photo in an evidence bag, and requested the sheriff have a deputy drive it to the MSP Crime Lab in Lansing for fingerprint analysis. The sheriff advised Colton was not a suspect, but rather, one of the good guys, so why did Dirk want his prints analyzed? Besides, his passport checked out clean in the LEIN (Law Enforcement Information Network) data base. Actually, there was no record of him. This wasn't uncommon as he claimed he was originally from Italy besides they saw no reason for a check through Interpol. Afterall he wasn't being charged with anything.

Dirk told the sheriff he didn't think he was a bad guy, but simply was concerned about a few things regarding him. He felt he was too clean, not even showing any history of ever receiving a traffic ticket. The sheriff relented and sent the deputy to the lab with the prints.

Dirk Smith's hunch paid off, as Colton Bishop was not in the system, but one of the computer techies at the lab did some extra checking. He found what appeared to be three instances in which there were ghost tracks in the Interpol database, that indicated three suspected matches of the submitted prints were erased. The techie only came across this once before in his career, and later learned through a back-channel source, that those particular prints belonged to an Israeli Mossad agent.

Dirk doubted that Colton was a Mossad agent, but believed he was backed by a powerful government organization of some sort. It was too much of a coincidence that he just happened to run into the Devil's Dungeons members twice.

Maybe Colton Bishop was a deep-cover FBI agent trying to prove his mettle to the gang leader so as to get recruited. Sure, he beat up some of the members pretty bad, but he didn't kill any of them. What better way to get noticed by the leader? Before he could continue this line of thought Dirk's iPhone vibrated indicating he was getting a call from the Oceana Sheriff Department.

It was the sheriff himself telling him that the girl, Allison, he hoped to meet was at a foster family house in an adjacent county and wanted to talk with him. He jotted down the address and said he would head over there soon. The sheriff also told him about the circumstances of them finding the girl at the church and once again Colton was there. He offered to have a deputy go along with Dirk, but he declined.

Dirk also neglected to tell the sheriff about his suspicions of Colton Bishop, which were getting stronger by the minute, especially since the gang leader had now sought him out.

Hopefully, the interview with the girl would get him enough probable cause for an arrest warrant against Lucas Sledge, before Colton tried to steal his arrest from him. The bureau was famous for that, swooping in after local law had already made a case, then taking all the credit. Not this time, thought Dirk. Not this time.

Chapter 24

LUCAS WAS AT THE CLUBHOUSE bar. He poured himself a double shot of Jim Beam and promptly drained it. Sumo passed him a ceramic bowl filled with Blue Dream. Sledge inhaled deeply, holding it in for several seconds before exhaling. "Damn that is good shit," he exclaimed while reaching for his bottle of Budweiser.

"So, what is the plan boss? We can't just let those cops get away with screwing with our bikes like that," said Sumo.

Lucas thought a moment. He had wanted to stay low on the radar and milk this area for all it was worth for a few more years, but the cops had crossed the line. Besides, in a few weeks everything would probably change for him anyway. He was destined for far greater things than Vice President of the Michigan Chapter of the Devil's Dungeon.

He decided it was time to step it up several notches with the cops and this cocky punk-ass cook. Something didn't feel right about him. He was more than a cook, that was for damn sure. Lucas could smell a cop a mile away, and this guy filled his nose with a strong stench of pig. Possibly an undercover cop. It didn't matter. If the cops and the cook wanted a war, he would give them one.

"I'm done pussy footing around here. It's time to show these assholes who is in charge. Nobody fucks with our bikes without serious payback! I want all hands-on deck in 15 minutes. Time to formulate a battle plan," replied Lucas, who then poured himself another double shot of Beam.

Sumo waddled out the back door to sound the air-horn; at nearly 400 pounds all he could do was waddle. The horn was attached to their flagpole and was stolen from a firetruck. It could be heard a ½ mile away. Two blasts were the universal call to haul ass inside for a meeting.

Less than 10 minutes later, all sixty-one members were present, with the exception of the three in jail. Sack was last inside as he was still trying to learn to use his crutches. AC/DC Highway to Hell blared over the stereo.

"Someone turn the damn music down and listen up, bitches," Lucas ordered. Once the music was shut off, he continued, "If these dumbass cops want a war, we'll give them one. No one is going to mess with our bikes without a serious shit storm coming their way." The assembled members cheered and stomped their boots on the wood floor.

"As all of you know, the local law here is starting to mistakenly think they can fuck with us. We are going to soon show them how wrong they are. Starting tonight we will show them who is in charge here," Lucas shouted.

There were more cheers and shouts of "hell yeah" that echoed about the clubhouse.

"Alright, alright, quiet down," Lucas said." We are going to destroy every police car in this town. And, we are going to kick the living shit out of this punk-ass cook that put our guys in the hospital. When we are done with him, he'll be in the morgue or damn close to it."

It took Lucas several minutes to quiet down the shouts of support and encouragement. "Ok—now listen up, because this is how we're going to do it!" A half hour later Lucas finished detailing his plan. He ordered everyone to be back, and to be mostly sober, in four hours.

As Linda was walking past, he grabbed her arm and said, "Stick around a minute."

She stopped and stared at him. She hoped he didn't want to fool around as she was still tired from her time with the deputy.

"You did great last night, but I need you to do a couple real important things for me today. If you come through, which I know you will, I'm going to do something real special for you." After ten minutes of hearing him out, Linda assured him she could handle it. "You're one special lady, Linda. I'll owe you big time."

Linda walked out of the club and called Deputy Nowak on her cell. Hopefully, things would work out, or he wouldn't live to see the next morning. She kind of liked him despite him being a cop and all.

Chapter 25

DETECTIVE SMITH FOUND the house without a problem, thanks to his GPS. The drive was just over an hour and was much better than driving around his Detroit precinct. Instead of drug houses, low-income housing, and other abandoned properties, he saw a multitude of trees, displaying their fall colors. Instead of weaving around drunks and crackheads, he had to brake numerous times for white-tailed deer and wild turkeys darting across the road. Not that all of his town was like that, but his precinct was in one of the worst sections of the city.

Detective Smith pulled into the driveway that his GPS informed him was the right place. He admired the two-story ranch style home with envy. It was surrounded by a variety of pine trees and he spotted a small lake behind it. A lone fishing boat was secured to the dock. Damn, I sure could get used to living like this, he murmured to himself.

The sheriff had called ahead to let the family know he was coming. They were still security conscious enough to ask to see his credentials. Afterwards, they showed him to a private den with a small wood stove, bookshelves, and comfy overstuffed chairs. The missus brought him a mug of coffee then excused herself.

Allison entered a few minutes later. He was struck by her confident gait and look. He expected a scared, little, thirteen-year old girl, but instead was looking at a confident young woman.

"Hi. I'm Allison. I have a lot to tell you."

She shook his hand with a firm grip then sat down in a chair across from him riveting him with a steady stare.

"Nice to meet you, Allison. I'm Detective Smith, with Detroit Homicide, but, please, call me Dirk."

"Ok, Dirk. My brother killed Father Matthews, then set the church on fire," she said without preamble.

"Did you see this?"

"No, but I was at the church that morning. I went there a lot. Father Matthews didn't know I was sleeping in a confessional when my brother came looking for me. I heard him threaten father while I was dragged outside by Whacko."

"Whacko?"

"Yeah, he isn't wrapped too tight, hence his club name. Anyways, while I was outside waiting with Whacko, my brother came running out a few minutes later telling us it was time to haul ass. I saw on the news the next day about the church burning down and Father Matthews being killed."

"Allison, will you testify to this? Tell your story in court?"

"Yes, sir, I will. And my brother killed one of his own guys two days ago. Shot him in the head. I saw that one."

Dirk let out a sigh, "Where did this happen?"

"In the clubhouse."

"Did you tell the sheriff that yet?"

"No sir, but I will if you want."

"Allison, you are a very brave young lady."

'No, I'm a coward, but I'm working on being braver."

"Not in my book, you aren't. You sit tight a few minutes; I need to make some calls. I'll be right back."

Dirk exited the home and started working his cell. After twenty minutes he returned to the den.

"Sorry to keep you so long. I'm getting some paperwork faxed over to the sheriff's department. I will need you to sign a few things. Affidavits is the fancy term. From these things I will get an arrest warrant for your brother, and then we'll pick him up. Are you ok with that?"

"Yes, sir. The sooner the better."

"Ok, problem is the courts will be closed for lunch soon, so I doubt I'll have everything ready until tomorrow morning. You will be safe here until then, as no one but us knows you're here. I'll be back by 9am. Ok?"

"That's fine; I like it here."

"Ok, I'll see you in the morning. And, you are not a coward. You are a very brave young lady."

"Thank you," Allison said.

Dirk spent a few moments talking with the foster parents telling them he would be back first thing in the morning and for them not to venture out until then.

They assured him they would stay put until he said otherwise.

Chapter 26

COLTON HAD SPENT MOST of the stormy day in prayer and meditation on a deserted stretch of sandy beach that he had walked to straight from the diner. Fortunately, when it started raining, he was seated on a picnic table that was covered with a small corrugated roof. It certainly wasn't the Italian Riviera, but it was still a beautiful beach. He often found himself drawn to vast expanses of water when he needed to think and plan. It helped clear his mind and organize his thoughts.

He seemed oblivious to the storm surrounding him. He was seated atop the picnic table, with his shoes resting on the bench section, gazing far out to the horizon but focusing inward. Despite his outward appearance, he was fully aware of everything around him.

The wind was blowing hard out of the west, dark black storm clouds hovered ominously above the rough white-capped water, with jagged bolts of lightning occasionally streaking down towards the lake below, like random mortar fire on a field of battle. Huge waves smashed against the defenseless beach spewing foamy spray several feet into the air.

Colton thought of his religious studies professor, Father Adalardi, who had once told him that Satan, and his evil army, rode bolts of lightning to arrive on Earth. At some point, Colton heard Botis taunting him, challenging him, ridiculing him. It was always like this, in every single assignment, just before the confrontation, the spirit taunted him. Not in the physical realm, but in the spiritual. At times, these moments were almost worse than the eventual physical confrontations. Colton had still not come to terms, or close to full comprehension of the other realm.

Botis was a powerful and formidable enemy. Colton felt his power and shuddered. Doubt began to enter his mind; perhaps he should have asked the Controller for one of the other four to accompany him. They were all more comfortable in the spiritual realm. Colton still struggled with this aspect.

Perhaps he wasn't ready for this task, but it was up to him. The others were needed at the Vatican, especially with the recent attack. Botis seemed stronger than any of the others he had faced before. He fought off the negative thoughts and prayed feverishly for the strength he would need, both physically and spiritually.

Colton knew the time to act was at hand. It wasn't any direct conscious decision on his part, but rather, an almost intuitiveness of what was required of him in the immediate future. He stared blankly at the rough surf, watching an abandoned beach ball being tossed violently about by the waves.

A sudden loud thunderclap snapped Colton out of his trance-like state. He glanced at his rugged Swiss military watch and was surprised to see that over four hours had elapsed since he first sat down. It was a few minutes before six o'clock. The worst of the storm had passed and only a light drizzle remained.

Colton stood, stretched, and turning up his collar on his leather jacket jogged back towards the main street. He was as ready as he would be for Botis, but first, he needed to straighten things out with Maggie. Her bungalow was two miles away. He was going to be seriously late. He debated about simply running down the beach the whole way, but the sand would make for slow going, so he continued toward the asphalt road a hundred yards away.

His mind was reeling. What was he going to say to her? He had not felt this way about anyone in a long time. He could easily see himself falling in love with her. He could only hope that she would understand. He had no illusions that they had any type of future together, but that didn't make it any easier.

He was jogging alongside the road, about a half mile from Maggie's home, when a black van suddenly stopped adjacent to him with the Devil's Dungeon design stenciled on the side. The passenger door slid open, the obese biker from the church earlier that morning said, "Sledge wants to see you. Get in."

"Have we met before? My mom always told me not to accept rides from strangers," Colton remarked.

"Funny guy. You pissed off Lucas really bad and busted up my kid brother, Sack, and I'm not real happy about that," replied Sumo.

"Ok, I can see the resemblance now, same big ears and ugly face, but wow, you really need to join your brother in the gym more often."

"Get in smartass, 'cause if you don't, I'll call Rosco, who is sitting just down the street from your blonde bimbo's house. He did seven years in the pen for rape. He's especially partial to blondes." Sumo was holding up a cellphone. "Oh, and the cop that was watching her house just got a bullshit call about a serious accident 10 miles away, so he'll be gone a while," Sumo smiled widely.

Colton recognized the driver of the van as one of the bikers that was with Sack yesterday. Two others sat in the farthest back of the three rows of individual, side-by-side, seats. A rough looking, younger woman was in the front passenger seat. He liked the odds, only 5-to-1, so he got in.

"That's a good lover boy, now shut the door!" ordered Sumo.

Colton did so, then turned to his left so he was facing Sumo and could keep an eye on the other occupants as well.

"The woman said, "You are not nearly as big as I had pictured you."

"I get that a lot," Colton remarked before turning his attention back to Sumo.

"Sumo—wow, all you guys have such cool names. Do you walk around at night in just a diaper with your belly hanging out?"

Despite themselves the other occupants laughed heartily at this.

"Shut up. Sit back and enjoy the ride."

"Seriously, you should consider a weight loss plan. Your BMI is way above the average."

"I said shut up."

"You can barely imagine how terrible a mistake it would be to harm Maggie in any fashion," Colton said in a matter-of-fact tone.

"Really—well, as long as you keep cooperating, we won't have to worry about that, but you do something stupid, and Rosco is turned loose on blondie."

Colton lived by simple mottos. One of his favorites was a quote by Teddy Roosevelt that went something like, there is nothing worse than to hit softly. If you decide to hit—hit hard!

As Sanchez, the driver, began a U-turn in the roadway Colton said to Sumo, "You made a serious mistake. You should have already had Rosco inside Maggie's house."

"Really and why is—"

Before Sumo could finish his question, Colton leaned forward and delivered a straight jab to the middle of his throat. Not hard enough to collapse it, but damn near. The obese man's eyes bulged as he struggled to inhale air.

Colton quickly pivoted to his left, and while leaning over the rear seat, delivered a punishing right hook to the biker's jaw seated directly behind him. The audible "pop" was heard over Sumo's wheezing, who was now gasping for air like a carp out of water. The other biker lost consciousness immediately and would be eating through a straw for a month.

The remaining guy in the rear seat, a middle-aged gray-haired guy that resembled Alice Cooper, was scrambling backwards, frantically trying to stay out of Colton's reach, but Colton, half out of his seat now, delivered a powerful backhand to the side of the guys face, following up with a palm strike to his forehead. The last blow caused the man's head to impact the rear window with such force it shattered. He was now also unconscious.

"You asshole," screamed the female biker from the front passenger seat. She was now out of her captain's chair in a crouch facing the rear section, holding a long, thin knife in her right hand. She had crazy eyes and a dozen silver piercings scattered about her eyebrows, nose, and lips. She resembled a punked-out version of Janis Joplin.

"I'm sorry, you must have really liked that window," Colton said.

She lunged forward slashing, from right to left, at his neck. Colton instinctively leaned backwards but was stopped short by the seat. The blade cut easily through his leather jacket slicing into the top of his shoulder, opening a several inch gash.

Colton continued to track the blade's movement with his left hand, then with the speed of a striking rattlesnake, grasped the woman's wrist just below the knife. With a vice-like grip, he hyperextended her wrist while locking her elbow with his other hand.

"Sorry, but I'm an equal opportunity fighter," Colton said while snapping her wrist like a piece of dry driftwood and dislocating her elbow. The blade dropped to the floorboard. She began to utter a high-pitched scream, but Colton ended that quickly as he drove his right elbow into the side of her head, rendering her unconscious as well. "Sleep tight," he said.

Only fifteen seconds had elapsed since the melee started. The driver, Sanchez, was cursing repeatedly while still driving down the road. Sumo was still making weird sucking sounds trying to get ample air.

Sanchez suddenly yanked the wheel hard to the right and slammed on the brakes. The impact flung Colton forward into the dashboard, between the captain's chairs. His injured shoulder took most of the impact with blood spattering onto the window from the fresh gash.

"You bitch," yelled Sanchez as he threw the van in park then lunged on top of Colton. Sanchez was thin, but wiry. He was trying to put Colton in a chokehold. Colton quickly tucked his chin down into his chest. Sanchez anticipated this and hunched in closer to try to gain leverage.

Colton suddenly snapped his head back into Sanchez' forehead momentarily dazing him. Colton twisted his torso to the left and brought his arm around Sanchez' neck, quickly wrapping him up in a chokehold. He squeezed until Sanchez could barely breath.

"Is Rosco really waiting down the street from Maggie's house?" Colton hissed in his ear.

"Yes!" Sanchez managed to say.

"Is anyone else with him?"

"No. No one, I swear," Sanchez squeaked as he fought for air.

"What is he driving?"

"His Harley, man; what else?" wheezed Sanchez.

"Ok. Nap time."

Colton continued the pressure until Sanchez went limp. He shoved him unceremoniously into the back seat, on top of the girl, next to Sumo, who was still frantically attempting to inhale air. His face was turning blue and he was clutching his throat with both hands.

Colton settled into the driver's seat, did a fishtailing, tire squealing, U-turn, and gunned the van towards Maggie's Street. Five down in less than a minute, not bad he thought, but a little slow. He took several deep steady breaths to try to slow down his heartbeat and breathing, which were both working in overdrive from the adrenaline dump that the fight-or-flight response caused.

Two minutes later, Colton was turning the van off the main road onto Maggie's quiet street. It was almost twilight; even so, he easily saw the Harley parked off to the side of the road with a rider astride it, facing away from him. Colton mashed the gas pedal to the floorboard while veering partially off the roadway.

Rosco still astride his Harley, half turned towards the sound of the rapidly approaching van. The Harley was a classic chopper style with an award-winning custom paint job. Colton saw the biker's eyes go wide like a deer caught in headlights. He made a good-hearted effort at scrambling off the bike prior to impact but didn't quite make it.

The right front third of the van squarely impacted the rear tire of the bike launching it several feet into the air before it crashed back to the road. The grating sound of metal against asphalt filled the air. Sparks shot from the pavement like fireflies.

The initial impact knocked Rosco up, and onto, the van's small hood. His right shoulder and head smashed into the passenger side of the front window. He somersaulted off the side of the van and rolled into the grassy, front yard of a vacant cottage next to Maggie's home.

Colton jammed on the brakes. The van skidded to a noisy stop. Colton was out in a flash. Rosco was on all fours attempting to stand. "You may want to consider wearing a helmet next time," Colton said.

"I'm fine, asshole," Rosco responded while still on all fours.

"I wasn't talking about the accident," Colton said and kneed him hard in the side of the head. Rosco crumpled to the grass.

Colton dragged the unconscious biker over to the van. Sliding the side door open, he hefted Rosco up, and in, piling him on top of the others before slamming the door shut.

"My God, Colton! What is happening? Are you all right?" Maggie was running down her driveway towards him. She was in near hysterics. "You're bleeding." She gently felt around his shoulder. Colton grabbed her firmly by both shoulders. "Listen to me. I'm fine. It is time to end this with these guys. Get in your car and drive. Do not stop until you are somewhere in Ohio."

"But, you can't fight them all," Maggie pleaded.

"Hopefully, I won't have to, just Botis."

"Who?" asked Maggie.

"I'll explain later. You have to go now. Get a hotel room somewhere in Ohio, and don't come back until I call you? Do you understand me?"

"But what about the diner or the police..."

"Maggie! Colton yelled, his eyes narrowing. "You have to do this. They were coming after you. Please do it now. Do not pack, just leave—hurry. Please, trust me."

Maggie didn't reply, but instead, nodded her head in understanding. She suddenly grabbed his face and kissed him hard on the lips. He tried to pull away after a few seconds, but she held him firmly in place. She abruptly broke away and said, "Be careful, Colton." She then ran back towards her house.

The sweetness of Chardonnay lingered on his lips as did the fragrance of her perfume. He looked after her a few seconds, before climbing into the van's driver's side, checking first that all occupants were still incapacitated. Sack's brother, Sumo, was still gasping for air and looking at him for help.

"Man up. Your trachea is only half collapsed. You'll probably live," Colton said.

Maggie was right. He couldn't fight them all and expect to live. He needed help, but that would have to wait. The groans and moans from the injured, half-conscious passengers were not unlike the whimpers and barks of captured dogs from an animal warden's van. Unlike stray dogs, Colton did not plan on euthanizing the bikers, although the thought did cross his mind.

He U-turned the van and headed back towards town.

Chapter 27

A FEW MILES DOWN THE road Colton pulled the van up to the volunteer fire department double-bay doors; luckily, a few pickup trucks were parked in the lot. He had hoped someone would be there. The fire station was much closer than the hospital, and Sack's brother, Sumo, was turning a dark blue. Colton knew most firefighters were also paramedics and would be able to stabilize the injured gang members until ambulances arrived.

Colton hopped out of the van and walked quickly over to the bay doors depressing a black button labeled "For After-Hour Assistance Please Press." A few seconds later someone responded, "Can I help you?"

"Not me, but there are several people inside a van parked outside the bay doors that need help. They were involved in an accident and require immediate medical attention."

"Ok, we'll be right out. Were you involved in the accident?"

"Actually, I was the accident," Colton replied truthfully. He then jogged back towards the main road, as he didn't have time to field any other questions or wait for the police. He was standing on the side of it with his thumb out for less than two minutes when an older maroon Jeep Cherokee drove by him. Its headlamps washed over him as it passed. The brake lights flared before the vehicle finally pulled over and stopped just a few yards ahead.

Colton jogged over to the passenger side door. Upon opening it, he was surprised to see a 70 something, gray-haired woman alone in the car. A strong scent of cheap perfume wafted out towards him as though the woman had bathed in it.

"Well, are you getting in or not?" asked the older woman.

"Um—sure," Colton replied as he slid in and closed the door. LeeAnn Rimes was singing a classic Patsy Cline tune on the radio.

"I know you're probably shocked that I'm picking you up, but at my age, honey, I'll do whatever it takes to get a handsome young man in my car," the woman said as she looked over her left shoulder then smoothly accelerated while merging back onto the highway.

"Why thank you, but you really shouldn't pick up strangers, especially nowadays," he said.

"To be honest, I never have before. If you would rather, I can stop and let you out," the feisty older woman snapped back.

Colton laughed. "No, please don't. I really do need to get back to Pentwater as soon as I can. I know it's only a couple miles. I would usually walk, but I'm in a hurry."

"I'm Nancy. I'll get you there no problem. I'm on my way to the casino farther north."

"Why thank you, Nancy. I'm Colton. You don't happen to have a first-aid kit, do you?"

"I sure do. In my trunk. Are you injured?" asked Nancy with genuine concern in her voice tinged with a touch of anxiety.

Colton was thankful once again for his needs being met. Things like this happened to him all the time. During an assignment it seemed that the greater urgency for his needs, the easier those needs seemed to be fulfilled.

"Yes, but nothing too bad. I cut my shoulder and I could use some gauze and a bandage," Colton said, as he felt the warm blood seeping down his arm and chest underneath his jacket and shirt.

Nancy started to slow down and pulled over.

"No. Please don't stop now I'll get the kit when you stop at Pentwater. I really do need to get back there as soon as possible."

Nancy looked at Colton and smiled then depressed the accelerator. "You know, now you are starting to worry me just a tad. An injured guy hitching a ride in the dark, in a hurry to get somewhere. And, worst of all, not asking to go to a hospital."

"Nancy, I swear to you, I'm not a threat to you."

"I believe you sweetie."

They drove on mostly in silence. LeeAnn finished her song and Trace Adkins started crooning a tune about taking his daughter fishing. Three minutes later Nancy pulled into the south end of town.

"This works for me," Colton said and started to open the door.

"Well, it doesn't work for me. Shut the door. I'm taking you to that gas station parking lot over there, and then I'm going to take a look at that cut of yours."

"That really isn't necessary. If I could just borrow some gauze and bandages."

"Nonsense. I'm a retired surgical nurse. At least let me bandage it for you."

Once again, Colton realized his needs were being met. He said a silent prayer of thanks as he pulled the door shut. His shoulder was throbbing and aching badly.

Nancy pulled to the far corner of the parking lot where she retrieved her first-aid kit from the trunk. She instructed Colton to remove his jacket and shirt. She was shocked to see the amount of blood soaked into his shirt, and the seriousness of the wound. "You need to get to a hospital and get this stitched up. You've lost a lot of blood."

"I will, but later. Please just bandage me up as best you can for now," pleaded Colton.

Nancy spent the next few minutes expertly cleaning his wound and dressing it. She bandaged it well and secured it with lots of tape at Colton's urging. Colton left off his bloodied shirt but shrugged on his leather jacket and zipped it close. Nancy handed him four Ibuprofen. "Take these. They're not prescription, but four of them will take the edge off the pain.

"Thank you, and God bless you," Colton said. He popped the pills dry, swallowing them.

Nancy smiled back at him oddly. "You're welcome. I just remembered a dream I had last night. I swear you were in it. I was in a church, and you were laying on the altar covered in blood. I tended to your wounds, but they were even more severe."

Colton gazed at her with a penetrating stare for several seconds before whispering. "Nancy, you have been away from the church far too long. It's time to come home again." Colton touched the side of her face then kissed her forehead gently.

"But, how did you know? How can you know anything about me?" Nancy asked incredulously

Colton turned away from her and exited the car. Prior to closing the door, he leaned back inside and said, "You might want to put some money on number 4 on the roulette wheel tonight," Colton said. He closed the door and jogged across the road towards his apartment building. The October night sky was now clear with a huge, yellow, full moon rising over the touristy city.

Several sheriff patrol cars, with red & blue lights activated and sirens blaring, roared past him as he entered the building. They were no doubt heading to the fire department to investigate how so many of the Devil's Dungeons sustained such a variety of injuries.

Once inside his apartment, Colton pried up the floorboard and retrieved his mini briefcase. He quickly powered up the phone and punched in a series of numbers; after three rings a man answered in German.

"It's Colton; I need to talk to the Controller," he said in German as well.

"He is in a very important meeting with the cardinal. Is your matter urgent?"

Colton sighed audibly into the phone. "It's extremely urgent, as it always is when I utilize this phone. Please, get him now." Colton snapped, but immediately regretted doing so as the young man was simply doing his job.

"Very well. Standby."

After a long two minutes on hold, the Controller finally answered with a simple, "Yes."

Botis is confirmed, and I need to intercept asap," Colton said.

"Give me a sit-rep," ordered the Controller.

Colton told him everything that had transpired since the church incident that morning, as well as what he needed and how fast he needed it. He was asking for a lot of resources to be put together in a very short time, but that was what the ultra-secret intelligence division at the Vatican was best at, allocating local covert resources quickly, anywhere in the world.

The Controller would gripe and complain about almost every request, but in the end, like a fine Swiss watchmaker, he would procure the many intricate resources that Colton would require to complete his nearly impossible task. All the pieces would come together, but unlike a fine watch, the parts were not being assembled to tell time accurately, but rather, to neutralize a threat as efficiently as possible.

When Colton was finished, the Controller said, "It sounds like a suicide mission to me."

"You said that the last time and all went well," Colton retorted.

"If you call everything going well with half a city block being leveled, two fatalities, twenty people injured, and you being admitted to the hospital, I suppose it did," retorted the Controller.

"This one could get a little messy too, but I'll try to contain it," Colton replied.

"Colton, do what you have to do to get this son of a bitch! I will take the heat as usual. His Eminence likes to complain, but if the mission is a success, we'll be fine. I'll get everything you need in place as soon as possible but will need a few hours. I'll touch base with you as soon as everything is ready. And Colton, be careful."

"Always," Colton replied then terminated the connection.

Colton now removed the handgun with the suppressor from the case, as well as the spare magazines. He expertly checked it for functionality then loaded it prior to tucking it into a pancake holster in the small of his back. He put on a fresh T-shirt and tossed the bloodied one in the shower. He shrugged on his leather jacket and placed the extra magazines in the pockets.

He hated the waiting. Once he was committed, he was like a caged animal. He needed quick energy and hydration. He ate two protein bars from his cupboard while washing them down with a bottle of spring water.

He was feeling better within a few minutes but knew he couldn't wait around the apartment as the deputies would want to question him about the van full of injured bikers. He was certain they wouldn't be too upset, but he didn't have the time to deal with that now.

He decided to head to the church and wait there until summoned by the Controller. He walked to his door, and upon opening it was startled by the Detroit Police detective, from Maggie's Diner, standing in the hallway directly in front of him. Colton noticed the gun in the detective's hand just as he was shot by it.

Chapter 28

DEPUTY JEFF NOWAK WAS having a banner day. He finished his shift at six o'clock. Fortunately, with all his seniority, he was able to work a permanent day shift. He didn't have to deal with all the fights and drunks that the night shift did. It had been a slow day just like he had hoped. He had spent half the shift talking with Linda on his iPhone. *Damn*, he thought, *I don't even know her last name.* She wanted to see him again tonight, and he sure as hell wanted to see her.

He called her just prior to his shift ending and asked where she was staying. He wanted to pick her up and take her to dinner at a new restaurant in nearby Ludington that the younger deputies raved about. Linda thought that sounded great but hesitated a few seconds before telling him what hotel she was staying at.

Most people would not have even picked up on the hesitation, but after thirty years in law enforcement Jeff noticed such things. She finally told him she was staying at the nearby Best Western. After terminating the conversation, he thought briefly about the hesitation but chalked it up to her simply being cautious despite him being a cop.

It was almost time to leave to pick her up. Jeff was at his cottage and had just showered. He generously splashed on some cheap cologne. He then opened his mirrored vanity grabbing a prescription bottle. He chuckled to himself as he shook out a blue pill into his hand. Maybe he should take two he thought; this woman was an animal. He washed down the pill with tap water then strode towards his closet to get dressed.

He was out the door ten minutes later looking like he should be going to a funeral instead of a date. That wouldn't shock anyone he knew as he was wearing his court suit—that was also his wedding suit, funeral suit, and, in fact, his only suit.

He hopped into his well-used Chevy Impala, tuning into a classic rock station while heading out towards the freeway. Bob Seger was halfway through his classic "Night Moves." Jeff was drumming the steering wheel to the beat and singing along.

He was really hoping that this woman could be the one. Some guys could be bachelors their whole life and be happy. Jeff needed constant companionship. He wouldn't admit it, but he needed someone to tell him what to do. It was the same with his job. He wasn't designed to be a leader, but he could be a productive deputy provided he was closely supervised. He just wasn't much into making tough decisions or having to think too hard. He had struck out three times in marriage and vowed he wouldn't commit to a fourth unless he was certain he found the right woman. He was hoping Linda might be that woman.

Ten minutes later he steered into the parking lot of the Best Western. Linda was smoking a cigarette just outside the entrance doors. She dropped it to the pavement and stepped on it carefully with the tip of her stiletto. Jeff stopped adjacent to her, leaned over and shoved the door open.

"You look great," he said, and he meant it. She had a short, pale green skirt with black nylons and a low cut, white, print blouse. She was carrying a thin, black, button-up sweater, no doubt for later, as the evenings were cooling down quick.

"Why, thank you. You look handsome yourself," she said, while sliding in next to him and pulling the door shut. She leaned into him kissing him deeply. "I really enjoyed last night," she only half lied.

"I hope you are hungry," he said as he steered out of the lot and merged onto the expressway.

"I'm always hungry, especially for dessert," She replied while winking at him.

Jeff had trouble focusing on driving as he continued down the street.

Chapter 29

HIS EMINENCE, DESPITE it being past 1 a.m., was deep in prayer in his Vatican apartment. This was his ritual for the start of the final stages of each mission. Colton and his assistants would need all the spiritual support they could get if they hoped to defeat Botis.

As an advisor to the only Pope in almost 600 years to resign, the current pontiff kept him in that position, as a personal favor to the prior pontiff. He was now on his fourteenth year in a Vatican position, and neither of the Popes knew about his most important contribution to them, the selection of "The Four" and their true purpose.

His Eminence believed the Holy Father had enough matters and concerns to deal with, and dutifully insulated him from those of the select group. Besides, if the true purpose of The Four were ever discovered, the Holy Father would need absolute deniability. Despite their best efforts to the contrary, at times the lives of some of their enemies were lost.

Although Catholicism did not preach surrender to an enemy, the proactive activities of The Four could be difficult for some of the followers to accept, especially when they were ignorant of the facts at hand. In part, the priests were to blame, his Eminence reflected. Especially the Americans, too many preached less and less about the devil, and his band of evil brothers, focusing more on the feel-good aspects of the Gospels.

His Eminence learned firsthand, years ago, just how strong the influences of the evil supernatural forces were. He knew then his sole purpose in life and had certainly fought the good fight on the front lines for many years, but that was a task for younger, physically stronger priests than he.

His Eminence allowed his mind to wander from his prayer to almost 55 years earlier. At 17 years old, Lorenzo Colosanti had already committed to a lifetime of service to his beloved church. He was due to leave for the seminary in a few months and was assisting a local priest in his hometown of Verona with various duties as part of an internship.

He would never forget the one evening that changed his life forever. It was only the fourth night of his internship when sister Margarite summoned him from a deep sleep by pounding on his bedroom door at 2:00 am. Groggily inquiring who was pounding on his door, and why, Sister Margarite told him Father Benvunito urgently needed his assistance in the church.

Young Lorenzo dressed quickly in his simple frock and sandals, then followed the surprisingly agile sister through the darkened stone corridor and staircase of the rectory to the church courtyard. Once outside they hurried across the darkened, cobble path to the side door of the church. Upon grasping the handle to the door, a sudden bone-chilling scream echoed from within. Lorenzo turned and gazed into the old nun's eyes.

Sister Margarite spoke resolutely, "Be brave, be strong, and above all pray unceasingly." And with that urged him forward while she herself began reciting a Hail Mary. Lorenzo cautiously opened the door and entered the candlelit interior of the cavernous cathedral.

He saw Father Benvunito standing on the altar with his arms outstretched as though administering a blessing to a beautiful young woman clad only in a white nightgown. Although the altar was three steps up from the floor of the main church, the woman was eye level with the father. Lorenzo at first thought she was over seven feet tall, but upon looking closer realized her bare feet were at least a foot off the floor. She was floating before the priest!

Lorenzo turned once again and looked at Sister Margarite for guidance. She stopped reciting her litany of prayers long enough to say, "Go! He needs you now. Do not fear the unknown, rather place your faith in God, and all will be well."

Lorenzo swallowed nervously and walked onto the altar. Father Benvunito appeared transfixed with the woman, but briefly acknowledged Lorenzo's presence and said, "Lorenzo don't look at her. Look at your feet. Now, get me some holy water. Do it now."

Lorenzo, gazing at his feet, could not help himself as his curiosity was too great. He looked at the woman's feet levitating only a few feet in front of him, and slowly allowed his eyes to wander upwards, despite his superior's admonition.

The beautiful young woman's dark brown eyes locked onto his. Lorenzo was captivated by the beauty of her face. The tip of her tongue parted her red lips and ran seductively across the top lip. The woman spoke, but a shockingly hideous deep voice emanated from her, "What have we here? A virgin. Perhaps father, you should sacrifice him to your God."

Lorenzo was immediately filled with anxiety and dread of a magnitude unlike anything he had ever felt before. His entire body began to shiver starting from his legs, and working upwards, until he was violently shaking.

"Lorenzo, turn away from her. Go now and get me the holy water," Father Benevento urgently pleaded.

Lorenzo's feet felt as though they were mired in heavy wet cement. He was barely able to move them or turn away from the levitating woman's gaze.

Sister Margarite grabbed Lorenzo's right arm and forcefully tugged him backwards. He turned towards the sister as he stumbled back. She slapped him severely across the face. "Go now and do as father says, do not look at her again," She scolded him.

Lorenzo's face was stinging from the blow, but the dread and shaking had left him. He nodded his understanding and ran to the opposite side of the altar to the marble, holy-water font. He grabbed a deep ladle used for baptisms, and after filling it, walked quickly back to Father Benvunito trying not to spill any despite his trembling hands.

Father Benvunito was commanding someone named Botis to leave the girl who was still levitating a few inches off the floor. He implored Botis to leave the woman while holding a large crucifix inches from the woman's face. Her pupils were now rolled upwards and only the whites of her eyes were visible as she trembled violently. "Lorenzo, throw the water on her now," Father Benvunito ordered.

"Don't do it, Lorenzo. If you do, I shall destroy you and all you hold dear," The woman responded in the hideous, deep, manlike voice.

"Do it now, Lorenzo, or the poor woman will lose her soul," urged Father Benvunito.

Lorenzo felt the icy coldness and shivering begin to return to his feet and slowly rise. A feeling of heaviness and doom filled him.

"Do it, Lorenzo!" screamed Sister Margarite.

Lorenzo did as instructed. He flung the ladle forward, its contents dousing the woman. She immediately collapsed to the floor. Lorenzo felt something brush roughly between the father and he but saw only a dark shadow. Spinning around he saw Sister Margarite knocked aside as well, then the side door of the church banged open, and the shadow melted into the night. Lorenzo was no longer cold or filled with dread.

• • • •

FATHER BENVUNITO COLLAPSED to his knees from exhaustion. Sister Margarite ran to him, but he waved her off telling her to check on the woman. Lorenzo stood in astonishment, riveted to the altar and forever changed.

His Eminence focused back to the present and prayed now for the priest in Grand Rapids, Michigan that he had contacted just an hour earlier. He tasked him with an extremely arduous assignment. The younger priest seemed confident, and capable enough, but so had the last one that was still being treated in a very private clinic in Rome. His parishioners were told he was on retreat. In reality, the clinic was trying desperately to save his sanity.

Chapter 30

COLTON FELL TO HIS knees while convulsing violently. Dirk kicked him in the chest, knocking him backwards into his room. He quickly stepped over his convulsing body and shut the door. The two, tiny darts, with thin copper wires trailing back to the Taser, were still embedded in Colton's chest.

When the five second ride of 50,000 volts ended, Dirk said, "Don't even think about moving or I'll give you a second ride." He was standing out of grabbing, or kicking range, with his finger still on the Taser's trigger.

Colton looked up at Dirk while still lying on his back. "That was intense! Now please, tell me why you did that," Colton said while breathing in and out deeply.

"Because, I'm not stupid. I know you're not a cook."

"You' re correct. As I've been telling everyone in this town. I'm actually a chef."

"Yeah, sure you are, and I'm Barack Obama," Dirk said.

"You haven't aged well since your presidency. May I at least sit up now?" asked Colton.

"No. Don't move. I need to know who you really are. I checked your prints from the photograph I handed you yesterday. Someone tried very hard to erase you from Interpol's database, but they left exit tracks. That means you are connected to some government organization in some way or are a serious hacker. Perhaps you are an agent, perhaps an informant, maybe a high-end criminal. Which one?"

"Ok, Detective. You must be very good to have learned that, so I won't bullshit you. For the record, I am a chef, but I'm also a part-time agent for a foreign government, but my assignment is highly classified. I'm on the side of the good guys here, are you?"

"Of course. If I wasn't, I would have shot you with my .45 instead of a Taser," Dirk said and smiled.

"Well, I suppose there is that to be thankful for," Colton quipped back followed by a lop-sided grin.

"I can understand classified assignments, but you have to at least prove to me you're one of the good guys. What is a foreign government's interest in the Devil's Dungeon?" Dirk asked.

"I'm only interested in their leader, Lucas Sledge."

"Shit! I knew it. Look, I have him dead to nuts. I'm arresting him tomorrow on a murder charge."

"Perfect, I will help you with the arrest, but I need him alive. And, you have to let me interrogate him before you take him away," Colton said.

"I don't have to let you do anything. If you're a foreign agent, my charges will supersede yours. You're on good ole U.S. of A soil now. But, if you're legit, and have some charges, you can have him after we're done with him."

"I don't want him. I just need to interrogate him. He'll be all yours."

"I know all about how some of you guys interrogate people. There may not be anyone left to take possession of."

"I can assure you that you have never seen an interrogation anything like we do," Colton acknowledged. "But, it's not what you're thinking. In fact, I suspect he'll be in much better shape after the interrogation than before it."

"That is difficult to believe. Now, give me someone I can verify your status with. What agency are you a part of?" Dirk asked.

Colton looked at Dirk for a long moment without speaking. Dirk started to get uncomfortable.

"Look, you have to prove to me who you are. For all I know you could be a Russian informant trying to work off being busted for selling a kilo of coke," Dirk said.

"I will help you, if you can trust me, we can work together," Colton replied.

"I'm doing ok without any help from you."

"Really, are you? You've been trying to quit drinking for a long time now. How's that working out for you without any help?" Colton demanded.

Dirk was taken aback by the abrupt personal question and didn't reply.

"Come on, Dirk. It's time to trust someone. Your mother told you on her deathbed that you needed to start trusting people. Start with me. I can help you kick that drinking problem. I know someone that can help you deal with that urge," Colton pleaded.

"How can you possibly know what my mother said to me when she died. I never told anyone that. Who the hell are you anyway?" Dirk said quietly. "You some kind of psychic?"

"Not exactly. I'm going to stand up now, and if you pull that trigger again you lose any chance of being sober. Now let's work together and take Lucas Sledge down."

Colton looked at Dirk for approval. He nodded almost imperceptibly. Colton shakily stood and yanked the darts from his chest.

Chapter 31

SHORTLY AFTER 1 A.M., when Nowak was snoring comfortably in his bed, Linda crawled out from under the blankets, then slipped into his robe and slippers. She grabbed her smokes and cellphone, then stepped out the front door. She was greeted by several hoots from a nearby owl and a spectacular full moon.

After lighting up, and inhaling a couple long drags, she called Lucas. When he answered she said, "It's Linda, Allison is staying with a Foster family at 6623 Robinwood Road in Calhoun County."

"Perfect. Is he suspicious?" Lucas inquired.

"I don't think so. I did just what you said. I got him talking about the girl. I acted all sad when he told me she was going to a foster family. I said I wanted to send her a card, as I was from a broken home too. He got me the address from his notebook. Apparently, he had to run her out some paperwork to fill out yesterday, so he had the information already."

"Ok—nice work. Can you get the other stuff too?"

"I already did. I slipped him what you gave me in his last beer. He is out like a light."

"Great job. I'll see ya soon."

Linda lit up another cigarette and stared into the dark night sky. She loved this area compared to Detroit. She had never heard an owl there. She was happy that Lucas was starting to trust her and confide in her. She wasn't long for the club. Since her boyfriend's death she had been planning on leaving. The clubs were for younger women. She longed for a quieter life now. She planned on taking a large portion of the club's treasury with her. They owed it to her. She hadn't touched a dime yet, but that would change soon.

She wasn't feeling the greatest about helping Lucas get his sister back. Allison was miraculously still a good kid. Linda would have to figure a way to help her as well. She finished her cigarette and went back inside to change into her clothes. The shitstorm was about to start.

• • • •

ALLISON LAY IN BED unable to sleep. It was almost 2:00 am and she was watching reruns of Stranger Things in her upstairs bedroom at her foster family's huge home. She liked the Hudson family as soon as she met them. They were both recently retired educators.

Mrs. Hudson was as bubbly as a glass of champagne. Mr. Hudson was quieter, but still fun. They didn't have any children of their own but had two friendly dogs; a collie and a corgi. Fortunately, Allison loved dogs. The corgi, Buster-Brown, had not left her side since she entered the home.

Allison's thoughts drifted to the previous day. The Oceana County Children Services had interviewed her for almost two hours after the church incident that morning. She was then taken to family court where a probate judge ruled, she would be placed in a foster home until Child Protective Services, and the police, finished their investigation into all the accusations she had made against her brother.

She thought about earlier today when the detective from Detroit finally interviewed her. Things were starting to move fast now. Allison still loved her brother, but despite her young age, was mature enough to realize she just didn't like him very well. A distinction that not many teenagers could make.

The Hudson's heeded the detective's advice and stayed home all day. Mrs. Hudson made a huge dinner of fried chicken with all the fixings. They watched a stupid comedy after dinner. Allison retired to bed early. She wasn't tired but figured if she feigned sleepiness at least she could watch what she wanted on TV in her bedroom.

Allison heard the chimes of the doorbell, shortly after settling on her bed. The dogs began barking loudly as they always did when the doorbells were activated. She slid out of bed and peered out of her window down at the driveway. A Sheriff's car was parked there. She heard Mr. Hudson answer the door and heard muffled voices.

After a few minutes she heard Mrs. Hudson knocking on her door and inquiring, "Allison are you awake?"

Allison opened the bedroom door. "Yes, I couldn't sleep. What do the cops want now?" she asked.

"I'm sorry honey but you need to go with the deputy right away. It seems your brother may have figured out where you are," Mrs. Hudson said in a slightly panicked voice.

"But, I don't want to leave here."

"I know honey; it's just until he's arrested tomorrow. The deputy is taking you to what they call a safe house. You'll be with the police all night. You'll be safe there."

Allison reluctantly gathered her few things and walked down the steps. As she entered the foyer, she was shocked to see her brother dressed in a sheriff's deputy outfit. He was clean shaven and cut his hair short like cops do. Mr. & Mrs. Hudson were momentarily turned away from him looking at Allison. Lucas had a finger to his lips imitating a "shh" sound with his left hand, while resting his right hand on the gun in his gun belt. He then pointed at Mr. & Mrs. Hudson. Allison received the message as clear as if he had spoken it. The corgi, Buster-Brown, was growling at her brother.

"Hello Allison. I'm Deputy Folger, but you can call me Mark. I'll be taking you somewhere safe for the night," Lucas said.

Allison didn't say anything. She stared in a daze at her brother.

"It'll be fine Allison. Deputy Folger will take good care of you," Mr. Hudson said.

"I sure will," replied Lucas with a broad smile.

The couple hugged her. Allison didn't hug them back. She walked wordlessly past Lucas out the front door towards the waiting police car. There was no sense running she thought. Lucas would surely kill them if she did.

Mr. Hudson asked Lucas, "Are we going to be safe? Are you saying that brother of hers, and his thugs may be coming here?"

"It's unlikely, but we will have a car posted at the end of your street all night and the other officers patrolling will be looking out for them as well. We doubt they even know about your place, but we received a tip they may, so we have to err on the side of caution."

"Well, ok. I guess I better load up my old hunting rifle just in case."

"Not a bad idea, sir. You can never be too safe. Well, goodnight folks," Lucas said and walked to the car.

Buster-Brown growled at the door with his ears laid back. "It's ok boy," Mr. Hudson said while patting the corgi's head, "He's one of the good guys."

Allison opened the passenger door of the cruiser, climbed in, and shut the door. The sound of it thudding closed sounded like a coffin lid being shut. Lucas entered the driver's side.

"Smart decision, sis. They seemed like decent folks. I'm sure glad you didn't make me kill them." He started backing out of the long driveway that sloped down to the road below. He was just about to back onto the roadway when an approaching car suddenly slowed down and pulled over to the shoulder, blocking his exit with its front end.

"Son-of-a-bitch," Lucas said when he realized the car was a Calhoun County Sheriff car. "Don't you move unless you want everyone dead," he said while glaring at Allison.

Lucas had the police radio on in the car. He did not hear anything unusual on it. His mind raced with possibilities. Did Deputy Nowak wake up early from his drug induced coma, and notice his uniform and car were gone? Or was this just a coincidence? Was the deputy just checking on the house and wondering why the Oceana Sheriff Office was here in his jurisdiction?

Either way this was not good. Lucas was reassured as the overhead lights on the car were not activated. A lone deputy exited the driver's side. Lucas did the same.

"Morning," Lucas casually said, as the young deputy approached him.

"Good morning," the deputy replied stopping a few feet away. "What are you guys doing out here so late? The sergeant told me to make hourly checks on the Hudson house tonight. Are you guys checking too? Kind of a long haul for you guys, isn't it?"

Lucas breathed a half sigh of relief. Hopefully, he could bluff himself out of this, if not, he would do what he had to do. "Actually, there was a last-minute change of plans. We are taking the girl to a safe house as we think her brother may know where she is."

"Seriously? Well, that's bullshit. No one notified us."

"Hey, I'm sorry, but it came from above my rank. I'm just following orders," Lucas said apologetically thinking the other deputy barely looked twenty-one years old.

"Sorry, I'm not upset with you, but we need to be kept in the loop on stuff like this. I'm Deputy Robertson. I'm fairly new and don't know too many of you guys in Oceana County. You have a card I can have?"

"A card?" Lucas asked.

"Yeah, a business card with your name; after all you're not wearing an ID tag. Like I said, I don't believe we've met before, have we?"

"No, no, I don't think we have. I'm Deputy Folger, just call me Mark. Um, I'm sorry, but I don't have a card. I just ran out," Lucas extended his hand and the deputy shook it.

"Nice to meet you," the young deputy said. "No problem about being out of cards, just give me your ID and I'll jot down the information and have my sergeant contact your supervisor about the mix up."

Lucas began to sweat. He had Nowak's ID card in his wallet, but he didn't look anything like him. What if the deputy knew Nowak? Lucas hesitated too long.

"Is everything all right?" the deputy asked

"Yeah, just fine, but I forgot my wallet at home."

The deputy subtly took a half-step backwards, and slightly angled his body away from Lucas. Lucas had spent a couple months cage fighting a few years back, and realized the guy was taking a defensive posture. He figured the young deputy was starting to suspect he was not who he claimed he was.

"I'll tell you what, humor me a second and raise your hands above your head," the young deputy said in a harsher tone than he had been talking in just a few seconds ago. While saying this, the deputy placed his hand on his gun grip.

Lucas decided to go on the offense. He knew the guy was new and obviously well trained. If this didn't work, Lucas would be forced to kill him, and the Hudson's would surely hear the gunshots, so he would have to kill all of them. Something he had no qualms about, but he didn't need the hassle now.

"What the hell are you talking about. Do you think I'm not a deputy? You think I just happened to rent a uniform, and order a damn squad car over the internet? You rookies are way too hyped up. I'm not raising my hands, and if you don't take your hand off your gun, I'll shove it up your ass! Now, I'm getting in my car, and backing out of the driveway, and if your car is still in the way, I'll ram the piece of shit! I'm sure your sergeant would love to hear about that."

Lucas stared defiantly at the younger deputy. He saw a brief flicker of uncertainty in the young man's eyes and took advantage of it by turning away from him and walking back to the squad car. Lucas entered the cruiser and slammed the door hard for added effect.

Once inside, he drew his handgun and rested it on his lap, but when he looked in his rearview mirror was relieved to see the deputy get back inside his patrol car and slowly back away from the driveway.

Chapter 32

THE CONTROLLER REPLACED the secure phone in its cradle. He rubbed both sides of his head, massaging his temples in small circles with his fingertips. His desktop was nearly spotless. His conscience not so clear. He had been up all night working his resources. His veins were probably pumping more espresso than blood through them.

It was 9 a.m. in Rome but only 3 a.m. in Michigan. He had assembled the small team that would be needed to assist Colton—the muscle portion at least. His Eminence was responsible for locating a properly trained priest nearby. Since the downsizing of the American military, there was no shortage of ex-military for hire, but finding them in such a short time frame, and close enough to get to Colton in a hurry, was the challenge.

The Controller was certainly up to the challenge. He had access to a vast database of mercenaries that only a handful of people in the world did. The problem was vetting them. Of course, he had touched base with prospective men as soon as Colton was operational. All were eager, especially when they learned of how much they would be paid. The unfortunate thing was Ricardo had not utilized any of them before. This was his first operation in Michigan. In fact, besides a short lived false-alarm mission in Chicago last year, this was the first mission in the Midwest.

It was a daring and probably foolish plan to storm the Devils' Dungeon clubhouse. They were woefully outnumbered, quite frankly, it seemed like a suicide mission, but Colton could not be dissuaded, instead insisting that time was of the absolute essence. Ricardo argued how that could be when his Holiness wasn't due stateside for three weeks yet.

Colton assured him Botis was becoming impatient, wreaking havoc in town as well as trying to kill him. Colton explained he needed to be on the offense, not the defense. The Controller finally conceded that it was probably best to strike soon.

In any event, the team was assembled and on their way to a hotel to meet with Colton soon. God, he hated this part. The waiting. It was time to call Colton and let him know where to rendezvous with his team.

• • • •

IT WAS 3:30 AM AND Oceana Sheriff Lt. Cairns was a little more than half way through his shift. So far, he thought, it had been a relatively quiet night, especially for a Sunday with a full moon. That was until a minute ago; while in his office attempting to catch up on paperwork, his desk phone rang. He now regretted answering it, as a seriously pissed off Calhoun County Sheriff Sergeant was chastising him about lack of prior notification for picking up a protected juvenile in their jurisdiction, as well as an insubordinate deputy.

Lt. Cairns had just told him to calm down when he suddenly noticed an odd flickering of light from outside, just below his second story window that overlooked the rear parking lot. He was used to the usual red and blue flashes from deputies testing their overhead lights prior to their tour, but the hue was orange and yellow, rather than red and blue.

He told the still upset sergeant that he would have to place him on hold a minute, which prompted a string of expletives. Cairns hit the hold button and walked to the window.

"What the hell?" he mumbled to himself.

A row of four squad cars, that were idled for maintenance reasons, were ablaze in the parking lot. Huge flames engulfed each car with heavy black smoke billowing upwards. One of the cars exploded and was propelled a few feet off the ground. When it landed, its doors blew off, as well as the hood.

Lt. Cairns instinctively flinched as a hub cap propelled from the blast, like a deadly Frisbee, it bounced off the window leaving a wicked crack in the glass.

"Judas Priest!"

He grabbed his portable radio from his desk and informed Central Dispatch of the fire advising them to announce a "10-33" to all officers out patrolling. This was an emergency declaration for all officers to return to the station asap.

Cairns jogged down the hall and pulled the fire alarm, then ran down the stairs and out the rear door. Two other squad cars now also exploded just thirty feet away. The concussive blast sent a wave of heat over him, toppling him backwards against the wall. He fell to his butt as glass and pieces of metal rained down around him.

Dazed, he regained his footing and ran around to the front of the building where his car was parked. As he rounded the corner, whatever doubt that this was not an intentional act, but rather, some type of freak accident, dissipated from his mind, as he saw his car completely engulfed in flames as well.

He grabbed his radio and let all the other deputies responding know that they were under some type of attack. He then unholstered his .40 caliper Smith & Wesson and approached the front doors that led to the lobby of the station. He noticed a standard size sheet of paper taped to one of the front doors. Sirens from the approaching fire trucks howled in the distance. Scrawled in black ink across the paper read, "An eye for an eye. Never mess with our bikes!"

• • • •

FATHER HUNT THOUGHT back to the call he received just a few hours earlier. The incessant, quiet buzzing of his cellular phone interrupted the young priest's typing of his letter of spiritual inspiration for the parish bulletin he was composing. He snatched the phone off his desk and frowned at the caller ID that displayed Vatican City as the origin of the caller. This was a first for sure. Intrigued and surprised, he accepted the call by attempting a hello, that sounded like a quiet cough, cleared his throat, and this time was successful at saying the ubiquitous greeting.

A heavily Italian-accented, elderly, male voice replied "Ciao—is this Father Hunt?"

"Speaking, um, who may I ask is calling?" A still puzzled Father Hunt inquired. Despite being of half-Italian heritage, he had only been to the Vatican twice in his life. He was currently a pastor of a cluster of three inner-city churches in Grand Rapids.

"Father Hunt, thank God you answered. I am Cardinal Lorenzo Colosanti. This can easily be confirmed by contacting the Vatican switchboard. I have an extremely urgent task I need you to do. It concerns your sub-specialty that you learned from Father Diago three years ago in Rome."

Father Hunt was now completely alert. "Yes, your Eminence, what do you require of me?"

"Please, listen carefully."

After the cardinal was done talking, he concluded by saying, "Be careful my son. As you know, this is an extremely dangerous task. I shall pray for you, and not stop doing so until I hear back from you. And equally important, do not mention this to anyone."

"You have my allegiance, as well as my discretion, your Eminence," Father Hunt replied just before the call was terminated.

He then logged into his desktop computer, and, shakily, queried the number for the Vatican switchboard. He dialed it and when answered inquired if a Cardinal Colosanti had left him a message. The operator replied, "He did. He also said to tell you to get busy as time is of the essence."

Father Hunt hurried nervously around the rectory, gathering the items he needed. Good Lord he thought, it had been three years since he had actually done this, and it was with the assistance of a veteran clergyman. That time was a success, but the pressure was not nearly as immense as it was now.

A cardinal was counting on him, and by the sounds of it the Holy Father as well, even if he didn't know it. Father Hunt was now hastily driving towards a hotel near Pentwater, still wondering what to expect when he arrived.

Chapter 33

COLTON RETURNED TO Det. Smith's hotel with him. He brought his mini attaché case along. Dirk seemed surprised when Colton had pulled it from the floorboards back at his apartment, but was not surprised at its contents, or alarmed, when Colton showed him the handgun with the suppressor in his waistband. Colton did not reveal the fraudulent ID's or passports to him. Dirk peppered him with additional questions, but Colton offered few answers.

For some reason, Dirk now trusted Colton. It wasn't solely because of what he said about his mother, or, the fact that despite it being after midnight, he didn't have the slightest urge to drink. When he thought about it later, it was almost a physical sensation that manifested itself into a mental attitude of complete trust in Colton. It was as if he felt like he had known Colton for years, and they were now as close as brothers.

Shortly after arriving at the hotel, Colton placed the sat phone on the desk. He explained he was waiting for a call from a superior authorizing him to proceed to the next level. Dirk argued that they needed to wait for the arrest warrant, but Colton argued it may be too late if they waited. Things were coming to a head. He felt it. It was a time for action not procedure. Dirk relented.

Colton stretched out on the leather sofa and tried to rest, but actual sleep was out of the question. A meditative rest was often all he required.

Finally, just after 3:00 am the sat phone chirped. Colton removed it from the case, walked into the bathroom, and spoke in rapid Italian. Dirk tried to listen but understood nothing. After ten minutes, Colton exited the bathroom and told Dirk that he had to meet with some people for a briefing at a nearby hotel in thirty minutes.

Colton explained that things could get a bit grayish regarding how they planned on picking up Lucas, especially without a warrant. He gently suggested Dirk stay behind. Dirk would hear none of it and insisted on going. Colton decided to leave early as he couldn't remain still any longer.

Dirk drove them up two exits south to the Fairfield Inn. Colton was surprised to learn from the clerk that several individuals were already in room 307. They were registered under his name. The motherly looking clerk eyed Colton suspiciously.

Dirk, sensing that she was becoming suspicious, stepped in front of Colton and flashed his badge at her.

"It's police business ma'am, but nothing to be concerned about," he assured her.

"Oh, thank God, you all don't look like drug dealers, but you never know these days."

"We understand. We just needed a quiet place to meet in a hurry."

"Take your time, you're paid for until tomorrow at 10 a.m.," she said while slipping them two plastic key cards.

They took the stairs and Colton knocked softly at the door. A gruff, cigarette-strained voice asked, "Who is it?"

"Samson. My Controller arranged this meeting."

"Samson!" Dirk whispered with raised eyebrows.

"Yeah, it's my code name," Colton replied sheepishly.

"Ok, but open the door slowly," the guy from within the room said.

Colton did so. A trio of gun barrels were pointed at him. He recognized each: A M&P sub machine gun, a Remington 870 police special 12-gauge shotgun, and an AR-15 assault rifle. The three men aiming each were spread out professionally in a semicircle about the room.

"Easy guys. I'm sure you were faxed a photo of me, and I gave you the proper response," Colton said as he slowly raised his hands.

"I can see you now, but I wasn't about to place my eye against a peephole and have my head blown off. You didn't hire amateurs," the oldest, and gruffest looking of the group replied.

"No, I sure hope not, for what you cost us," Colton said.

"I also have a friend you were not told about. He's a Detroit PD homicide detective. Please lower your weapons."

The other two looked at the older guy, obviously the alpha male; he nodded. They partially lowered their weapons. The muzzles now pointed slightly down and away from them, but ready to reengage in a millisecond, if necessary. Colton was impressed and reassured with the hired help. He waved out the door motioning Dirk forward. Dirk walked slowly into view. His hands raised.

"Damn. You guys brought some serious firepower," Dirk remarked after taking in the room with a casual glance.

The three smiled and nodded.

"Is the priest here yet?" Colton asked.

"Yep. He and the pig farmer are in the bathroom," replied the older guy. "Sounds like the start of a joke doesn't it. What exactly is going on here, anyhow? I suppose it's ok to have a priest on a mission for last rites and all, but a pig farmer?" the grizzled leader asked.

Colton walked over to the closed bathroom door and slowly nudged it open. A priest, in traditional black garb and white collar, was seated in the tub with his mouth, hands, and legs duct taped. Another man, wearing denim jeans, and a tan Carhartt jacket, with a soiled green John Deere ball cap was seated with his back to the priest in the same tub similarly bound.

"What's with the restraints?" Colton asked the team leader.

"Like I said, we're professionals. We're not about to take any chances," he replied, unapologetically.

"Okay but cut them loose now. We're all on the same team. We need to prepare."

Colton looked at the two men in the tub.

"I apologize, but, unfortunately, things will probably get much worse than this for you two today."

Chapter 34

COLTON HAD TO ADMIT, once again, the controller had come through in a big way. He surveyed the room, his gaze lingering ever so briefly over the assembled individuals an odd group to be certain: three former special-op soldiers, a priest, a pig farmer, and a soon to be retired DPD homicide detective.

"Ok—time to get started," Colton said standing in the small suite, at the head of a table with a dry erase board on it. A hasty, but accurate sketch of the exterior of the Devil's Dungeon Pentwater Clubhouse was depicted in red marker on the board.

"We suspect there are between 60-75 members inside the complex. Obviously, we are a bit outnumbered, so we will have to move quickly and with precision."

"Not a problem. Ricco; Jacks and I have had worse odds and lived to talk about it," remarked the older, well-conditioned, ex-navy seal captain, Mitch Sloan, who Colton had since learned was the team leader of the trio.

"That is exactly why you and your friends were chosen, Captain Sloan," Colton replied.

"Well, you were damn fortunate to find us on such a short notice," Ricco added.

Ricco was a short, stout, heavily-tattooed Latino, with a touch of grey sprinkled throughout his otherwise black crew-cut. He looked more like a hardened criminal than a prior bronze star recipient.

Dirk spoke up, "I still don't understand why we don't wait for the warrant and use about fifty officers to raid the place?"

"Because, I need Lucas Sledge taken alive. And, I can't guarantee that will happen with the local police handling it. We just do not have time to wait this guy out," Colton answered.

Colton looked at the three mercenaries. "Remember, keep casualties to an absolute minimum, and do not kill Lucas!"

"We can't make any absolute promise on that request; after all, we have trained our whole career to shoot to kill," grumbled Sloan.

"I understand your training, but understand me now, if he is taken alive your pay will double," Colton countered. "I want any, and all, casualties kept to a bare minimum."

Sloan arched his right eyebrow impossibly high then nodded his understanding, before draining the last of his black coffee from the paper cup. "Well then, if either of my men kill Lucas, I'll personally kill them."

Ricco and Jacks laughed at Sloan's remark, but Colton could tell it was a nervous laugh filled with uncertainty if their leader was jesting or not.

"Your employer must have mighty deep pockets," Jacks offered. The youngest of the trio, he resembled a forty-something California surfer, but he was still lean and mean. His Army Ranger days were not far behind him.

"You could say that. They own their own country," Colton replied.

"High-end drug lords; I knew it," said Jacks, "They all own a freaking island or country."

"No, not drug lords, in fact, far from it, but we digress," Colton said.

Dirk's cellphone began to beep, and everyone looked at him. He fished it out of his jacket pocket. He listened for a moment, then handed the phone to Colton. "It's your boss, Maggie. She sounds scared."

Colton snatched the phone from Dirk, chastising himself for not calling her earlier.

"Maggie, please tell me you are safe somewhere in Ohio?"

"Well now, if it isn't my good buddy the cook," said an ominous voice, that Colton immediately recognized as Lucas Sledge.

Colton attempted unsuccessfully to hide the emotion in his voice, "Let me talk to Maggie."

"Maggie, Maggie, Maggie. She sure is something. I can see why you like her so much. I can't wait to get more intimately acquainted with her."

Colton turned his back on the group and walked into the bathroom. Shutting the door, he whispered, "Listen to me very carefully. I know all about you Sledge. I know about your threats to the Pope, and I know you killed a priest. As difficult as this is to believe, I want to help you, not hurt you, but I can't do that if you hurt Maggie in any way."

Sledge was thinking fast. Allison, it had to be Allison. But how did she know? She must have figured out his password for his computer and read some of his e-mails. She must have read somewhere that the priest was murdered and told Colton all of this. His plan was getting screwed up fast. He needed to take care of this punk-ass cook sooner than later.

"Well now, you think you know everything about me, do you? Apparently not, because you said priest as in singular. I suggest before coming to Detroit you pay your respects to Father Carlos."

"Detroit? Father Carlos? What have you done now Lucas?"

"Only what needed to be done. Those old churches sure burn fast," Lucas replied coldly. You can fetch your gal at our clubhouse. We'll talk there—real soon."

"I'll be there in 15 minutes. If you hurt another priest, or Maggie, it would have been better for you had you never been born."

Lucas felt a cold shiver from deep within. He thought back to when he had stabbed the priest in Detroit several months ago. The priest had said the exact same thing to him as he was dying.

"You can't possibly be here in 15 minutes. You were not listening to me earlier. I said before you come to Detroit. We moved on. We're on our way back to our main clubhouse in Detroit. Be here before noon. I'll try not to hurt her too much before then. Come alone. No cops. I see or smell anyone else, and real bad things happen to her. Do you understand me, Cook?"

"I'm on my way. I can make you a deal, but only if Maggie stays safe," Colton half pleaded and immediately regretted doing so.

"Deal? We don't have a deal. I'm holding all the cards."

"Lucas—I'm serious. I'm on my way. Don't hurt her. Don't let Botis make you do anything else you'll regret," warned Colton.

"Just get here before noon, or you will be responsible for her never seeing 12:01." Lucas terminated the call.

Colton exited the bathroom and tossed the phone to Dirk. "Call 911 and get the fire department and the police to St. Michaels. I think it's on fire, and Father Carlos may be inside."

Colton turned to the others. "Change of plans. Father, you and Mr. Jones start driving towards Detroit in his rig. Call Det. Smith on his phone when you get there."

"Sloan, you and your men get me a helicopter that seats at least five, asap. I don't want excuses; I want a chopper in this parking lot in 60 minutes or less, even if you have to steal one from the hospital. Get it done. We're flying to the main Devil's Dungeon Clubhouse in Detroit."

Sloan whistled low and slow. "Not only can I get it done, but Ricco owns one and can fly the bird better than most. Is it set to go Ricco?"

"Sure is, Captain. It'll only take a few minutes to arm it. How does a couple hellfire missiles sound to you, Mr. Colton, besides the floor-mounted machine gun?" Ricco inquired.

Colton smiled. Once again things were being provided for him just as he needed them. He thought about the admonition from his Controller about keeping the mission on the low-profile side. His Eminence would not be happy if they blew up the compound in the middle of a major U.S. city.

"Ricco, as tempting as that is, let's leave the hellfires behind. Now let us rethink this plan, as I suspect there will be double the manpower in Detroit, but I need to make a call first."

Chapter 35

THE CONTROLLER TERMINATED the call from Colton and rummaged around in his desk drawer for a MS cigarette. He finally found one, lit it, and inhaled a third of it in one long drag. The lad was going to give him a heart attack, no doubt about it.

Ricardo had previously anticipated the eventuality that the main clubhouse of the Devil's Dungeon may have to be breeched. After all, it is not uncommon for someone to seek refuge where they feel the most secure.

Blueprints had been obtained, satellite imagery was viewed, police reports read—all concerning the main clubhouse. All of this had been arranged weeks ago. Despite this, he was anxious, as he always was when one of "The Four" was about to execute a nearly impossible task.

Ricardo was not in his position because of his connections or powerful friends. He was in his position because he was the best, by far, at what he did. He was anticipatory in nature. He knew what an agent in the field would require often before an agent did. He was a master planner that demanded total dedication from his small, but talented, staff.

Despite all this, he was nervous. He dragged deeply on the Italian cigarette again. Colton was basically planning to surrender to his enemies, in a heavily fortified compound, in exchange for one woman. And, somehow, he was planning to extract Lucas Sledge, alive, as well.

Damn Colton and his Delilah! Ricardo still had no doubt that Colton could terminate his adversary once inside, but that course of action was not the primary objective, although it may indeed have to suffice. What was the most troubling was that Colton may very well not make it out alive.

Agents were lost from time to time in lessor organizations. It was the nature of the job. Since the inception of "The Four," all were the original appointees, but too often Colton seemed to push the envelope as though he was looking forward to his demise. Yet, the battery of psychological tests and evaluations performed on him suggested otherwise. They all indicated Colton was near fearless yet maintained a strong desire to live, and to protect the holy father. His desire to protect others, even strangers, was off the charts.

The Vatican's head shrink, Dr. Kartaris, referred to him as the ultimate protector. He was fiercely loyal to upholding a moral code, not just for himself, but others as well. This coupled with his unmatched athleticism, his expert skills in hand-to hand-combat, as well as a proficiency in a variety of weapons, not to mention the inexplicable supernatural aid "The Four" at times seemed to receive, did indeed make him the ultimate protector.

Ricardo, the life-long atheist, mumbled his second prayer in a week. "If you truly exist, Lord, watch over the crazy lad."

Chapter 36

"THIS IS IT, LUCAS. No more bullshit," Ron "Whiskey" Banner admonished.

"But boss, let me explain," pleaded Lucas.

"Shut the fuck up. If you say another word, I will start a banishment hearing. Now sit down and listen." Lucas did as he was told. They were in Whiskey's office, inside the main clubhouse in Detroit. The threat of a banishment hearing from the gang did the trick. The Devil's Dungeon was the only family Lucas had now, besides Allison.

"We will take care of this cook when he shows up, but I'm not happy about the mess you made in Pentwater. You were doing so well there. Your Ecstasy sales alone were the highest in the state," Banner shook his head from side to side. "I don't mind a little heat, but if that cook goes to the cops, we are gonna have a whole shitload of heat. Not that they will ever try to come inside here. They are not that stupid, but they could harass the shit out of all of us when we are out and about," Banner continued.

"He'll come alone. I know this guy. He thinks he's a badass," offered Lucas.

"Apparently, he is a badass. He kicked most of your guy's asses, even several at a time," yelled Banner.

"Yeah, maybe, but I'm not scared of the guy. I can handle him; besides, if I had authorized firearms usage against him, it would not have gone this far. I didn't want any of our guys doing serious time for possession of a weapon, as the cops were all over us every time we rode," countered Lucas.

"If you could have handled him, you would have done so by now; that is why you came back, because you can't handle him."

"Whiskey, that ain't fair. I haven't had it out with him myself."

"Fuck fair, it's the truth. You'll get your chance to take this cook down if he shows up, but once he sees this place, do you really think he'll just waltz in the front gate, alone? He would have to be suicidal. We got over a hundred members inside now, and more on the way," Banner reasoned.

"He's a cocky bastard, but he likes the girl; I know that. I think he'll come."

"Well, we'll see soon enough. Now what is this bullshit about you killing Skunk?"

"Like I told you, Whiskey, he messed up bad. He turned all coward on the other guys. What choice did I have?"

"You are not judge, jury, and executioner, when it comes to a member! Never do that again without my consultation or a command vote, or you'll be out of the club. You got that?"

If Whiskey only knew how wrong he was, thought Lucas. He would never tell Whiskey about his plan to kill the Pope. He once confided to him about his repeated dreams concerning the messages he got from the talking dog with the horn in its head. Whiskey said it was just bullshit, drug-fueled dreams. Lucas knew better. He had received frequent messages from the dog until Botis finally revealed himself to him.

"Did you fucking hear me, Lucas?" roared Whiskey.

"Yeah, I heard you. Sorry, I guess I screwed up."

"Damn right you did. Do not let it happen again. So, when can we expect the cook, if he shows up?" Banner asked.

"Well, he has a solid three- to four-hour drive. It'll be a bit, but he'll show," Sledge said with conviction.

Chapter 37

ALLISON WAS LOCKED in a small, windowless room with Maggie. She lay face up on a twin bed gazing at the ceiling. Maggie was crying softly in the other bed across the room. She was bound and blindfolded when driven through the entrance a few hours earlier. Allison had since told her they were at the main clubhouse in Detroit, a place Allison was all too familiar with. She informed Maggie it was located in a repressed section on the outskirts of the city, with defunct businesses and blighted neighborhoods nearby. Unfortunately, it was an area largely ignored by the police.

It was a virtual fortress. Several years prior, it was a trucking company on just over seven acres, surrounded by a six-foot chain-link fence, capped with barbed wire. There was only one entrance, with a guard shack at the gate and a small lookout post on top of the building that was always manned. When actual gang members were not patrolling the perimeter, they had guard dogs roaming the grounds.

Maggie was crying at the overwhelming helplessness of her situation.

"I'm sorry my brother is such an asshole," Allison said softly.

Maggie didn't reply at first, but continued weeping. "What do you think he is going to do with me?" Maggie asked hesitantly.

"I don't know. He sure is pissed at your boyfriend, Colton."

"He's not really my boyfriend. He just worked for me. We never really even went out," Maggie corrected the girl. "I only knew him a few days."

"Well, whatever, but my brother is still pissed at him. I think he'll use you to get to him. Lucas doesn't ever stop until he gets what he wants."

"I'm sure the police will come for us soon."

"No, not here they won't," said Allison, vigorously shaking her head. "Whiskey, that's the president of the club, told me that cops tried to get in here twice before but didn't succeed. He said cops nowadays are too scared to try to get in here as it's too fortified. They have all kinds of weapons and even an underground bunker. The cops are scared of standoffs nowadays since Waco and stuff. Besides, no one knows we're here," Allison said matter-of-fact like.

"You really aren't cheering me up very much," Maggie said while wiping away tears.

"Sorry—we better get some sleep," Allison offered.

Allison fell asleep slowly, wondering why Colton didn't save her. She dreamed of him again and a talking dog with a horn in its head, like a demented unicorn. The dog bit Colton as he tried to save her and Maggie. Fire was all around them. Colton kicked the dog, but it only laughed at him and attacked more fiercely. The flames grew hotter. Colton was bleeding badly, his blood pooled on the floor, running like a river, away from his body to a nearby floor drain. His face became paler. He lay on his back, on an altar. He was holding the dog about the neck. Its massive incisors dripping saliva & blood onto his face.

A priest suddenly appeared and rebuked the dog. It left Colton and sprang for the priest's throat. The dog's face was now replaced with her brother's. Allison screamed and was immediately awaken only to discover Maggie was gone.

• • • •

MAGGIE FOLLOWED LUCKY Linda down a dimly lit hallway. Linda was carrying a black duffel bag.

"Why are you helping me?" Maggie whispered.

"Shh—just stay quiet and follow me."

Linda slowed as they approached a T-hallway. She stopped just short of the junction and leaned forward, looking both left and right. "It's ok, come on." She then took a right and headed for a door at the end of the hall. Once there she depressed the horizontal bar and gently inched the door open. "Come on, we don't have much time."

Linda and Maggie stepped outside into some type of large gravel parking lot. An eerie pale, yellow pallor, cast by the overhead lights partially illuminated the lot. A few cars and pickup trucks were parked there. Linda led Maggie to a shadowy spot near the corner of the building.

"There are two guards walking the fence line and another in a small tower on the roof watching monitors. When I tell you to, you run straight towards that part of the wall and carry that with you," Linda pointed towards an 8' section of a wooden ladder against the exterior wall nearby.

"Lean it against the fence and we'll climb up and over as fast as we can. You'll need this too." Linda handed her a bath towel that was rolled up.

"Lay this over the barbed wire then climb on top and jump down. You'll be ok as there is grass on that side. We'll be in a cemetery. Once there run like hell across it and keep running until you find help. You'll be on your own then as I got somebody who is going to pick me up, and he doesn't want to be responsible for anyone else."

"Why are you doing this?" Maggie asked. "And why couldn't we bring Allison?"

"I don't know. Lucas and Bannister will kill me if they find out, but it ain't right. He shouldn't have taken you. I mean I understand him wanting his sister back but not you, that was wrong. We will let the police know about Allison. They will find a way to help her. Lucas would never hurt her. Now, let's go," Linda said.

The headlights of one of the parked trucks nearby suddenly switched on. Maggie and Linda were completely illuminated. "Going somewhere, ladies?" Lucas asked.

Chapter 38

ON THE HELICOPTER RIDE across the state, Colton outlined the plan for the others. They spoke through headsets as the noise in the cabin was very loud. Ricco was flying a restored vintage Vietnam-era helicopter. The UH-1was painted black instead of the classic army green. Although it did not have any missiles attached, it did have a floor-mounted 7.62mm machine gun on one side.

Colton had a playbook for each of them that he assembled while waiting for them to return with the chopper. With the help of the hotel's fax machine, computer, printer, and a cooperative desk clerk, Colton had received blueprints, topographical maps, and street-view photographs of the clubhouse, and other intel from the Controller. He assembled these into a playbook for each member to study.

The matronly clerk was very impressed when Ricco landed the chopper in the hotel's parking lot. She told Colton this was better than watching reruns of "Cops" anytime.

Just prior to takeoff, Colton was relieved to learn from Dirk that Father Matthews was alive, but only because of the quick police and fire response. His church was a total loss due to the fire, but other than smoke inhalation he would be fine. Dirk had learned about the patrol cars being torched and confirmed that it appeared the Devil's Dungeon had left town as their clubhouse was empty. He was also told Allison was missing as was a patrol car.

Once the playbooks were distributed Colton spoke: "Sloan and Jacks will enter the sewer pipes through a manhole on the other block over here," Colton referred them all to a red X on page two, that displayed a street map of the surrounding blocks. "You will then follow the pipe east a hundred and fifty yards and rig a small charge of C-4 underneath the main hall here." Colton referred to another red X. "It will be set to detonate at exactly 6:15 am. When it does, you will be positioned fifty yards to the east, and blow a hole in the floor, at the exact same time, underneath a utility closet here. You two will then immediately enter the complex and look for Maggie & Allison. If you encounter Lucas, remember, we want to take him alive. Any questions thus far," Colton inquired.

The others shook their heads. Colton continued, "Ricco, you and Det. Smith will hover over the rear of the main complex at the same time. I'm told half of the hundred or so members on the premises will be sleeping in a smaller building about 50 yards southeast of the main building. Remember, they don't expect us for at least a couple hours. You and Smith need to keep them contained in that building so we only have to deal with roughly the same amount in the main clubhouse. I want complete chaos both outside and in but make certain it is chaos only for them. Ricco, are you sure you can navigate the chopper past all the overhead utility lines?"

"Not a problem," Ricco answered confidently

"And, you and Dirk can control the chaos you create—correct?"

"Roger that, can do," Ricco said. "And what the hell are you going to be doing while we're having so much fun—work a crossword puzzle?"

"Actually, I'll be driving through the front gate exactly fifteen minutes before the fun starts," Colton said.

The assembled group stared at him in disbelief.

"Sounds like a suicide mission for you, but ballsy for damn sure," Sloan said.

"I've been through worse and lived to tell about it," Colton replied with a wry half-smile.

"What in the hell is the priest going to do? Administer us our last rites?" Jacks asked.

"If necessary, yes, but he'll be waiting at a nearby, foreclosed church with the pig farmer," Colton replied.

"This is all too weird. And, what exactly is a pig farmer with a truckload of hogs doing here anyhow?" asked Jacks.

"Haven't you ever heard of their voracious appetite. Those damn hogs will chew up a dead man faster than you can go through a rack of ribs." Ricco laughed as did Sloan.

"As I've said before, none of you need to be concerned what the other members are here for or who the employer is. You are being paid quite well not only for the mission but your discretion and discreetness," Colton said.

"Copy that. We understand compartmentalization necessity," Sloan responded. His men nodded in agreement.

"Good to hear. Moving on. Sloan & Jacks you two are responsible for extricating Maggie and Allison after you blow the hole in the utility room floor.

Get them out safely, only then come back and help me extricate Lucas," Colton continued.

"If you can manage to stay alive that long," offered Ricco.

"Don't worry about me. It will only be about fifty against three inside. As long as Sloan and Jacks can handle ten each, I'll take the rest," Colton said confidently. "Remember, no unnecessary killing, especially Lucas Sledge."

"Define unnecessary for me," Sloan asked.

"Only kill those trying to kill you, but if it's Lucas, only wound him, if you can," Colton explained.

"Well, it sounds like a damn walk in the park to me," Sloan added dryly.

Dirk, who had remained silent, finally spoke, "If we make it through this, I'll buy each of you a Vernors and a Coney dog."

"Exactly what is a Vernors?" Colton asked.

"It's the best ginger ale you'll ever have," Dirk said.

"Really. All we get is ginger ale? I was hoping for a cold Strohs," replied Sloan.

"Don't blame me, blame him." Dirk laughed while pointing at Colton. "I haven't the slightest urge for anything stronger since I met him."

"Sloan and Jacks just get the girls out safe, then get back to the complex. We'll fly Sledge out with the chopper. If that is not feasible, we'll take him out via the sewers. Any questions?" Colton asked.

"Yes, one. What do we do when the cops show up?" Ricco asked.

"According to Dirk, we will be blowing the floors at shift change and any dispatch to the clubhouse demands a minimum of a six-car response. This will take at least 15 minutes and then they will just watch from outside the gate especially when they see all the chaos; isn't that correct, Dirk?"

"Correct! That is standard protocol. Then, they'll call for a special response team and by the time they arrive, if we're still there, we'll probably all be dead anyhow. But please, whatever you do, don't shoot any officers," Dirk replied.

"I expect us to be in and out by 6:30. And, as Dirk said, don't shoot any police. Any other questions?" Colton asked.

"Yeah, about a thousand but screw it. Let's just do this!" Sloan said.

Chapter 39

COLTON RODE THE HARLEY to the front gate of the clubhouse, stopping a few feet from it. Prior to arriving in Detroit, Det. Smith had contacted an informant of his who owed him a favor and asked to borrow his bike. It took a threat of exposing him as an informant to convince him to part with his beloved Harley, even if for only a few hours.

A leather clad, long-haired, whip-thin biker slowly emerged from the small metal guard shack on the other side of the fence. "Who are you?" He inquired through the chain-link fence gate.

"Colton Bishop. I'm here to see Lucas Sledge."

"Right. You're way earlier than we expected. You're the cook from Pentwater we've heard so much about. You sure don't look that tough."

"Never claimed to be; a guy with your physique scares me."

The emaciated biker didn't seem to get the intended sarcasm. "You better be scared cook. I'm a born and raised Detroiter."

"I'm practically pissing my pants. After all, you come from the same environment as Madonna and Eminem, who wouldn't be scared?"

Realization that he was being made fun of dawned slowly on the biker, but he eventually figured it out. "You think you're a pretty funny guy, don't ya asshole?"

"Why don't we skip the pleasantries. Lucas is expecting me. I suggest you open the gate and tell him I'm here."

The biker narrowed his eyes, then reached behind his vest and casually pulled out a sawed off, double-barreled shotgun. He clicked back both hammers, then leveled the nasty weapon at Colton. The two huge barrels were aimed directly at his midsection. "Stay right where you are and keep your hands on the handlebars, or I'll blow you in half."

"I'm impressed that you know fractions. If you blew me into four pieces do you know what fraction that would be?"

"Huh?"

"I didn't think so," Colton sighed. "Everyone should complete their basic education. It would be one-fourth, and if you reloaded again and blew me into twice as many pieces, what would that be?"

"Listen, you are starting to seriously piss me off—just shut the fuck up!"

Another man walked up from the shadows. "Relax Freak and quit bullshitting with the guy, just open the damn gate already." The second biker was a few years older, stockier, and bald. Despite the cool air, he was shirtless. A single gold earring adorned his left ear. His torso was covered in numerous tattoos that all blended together. It was obvious he liked weightlifting. Colton thought he resembled a dirty, grungier, Mr. Clean, from the American commercials.

The skinny biker reached into his left pocket with his free hand and hit a remote. The fence gate started to slowly retract, clanking and creaking as it rolled open. Colton remained on the bike with his hands on the handle grips as instructed.

When it was finally open, the stockier biker approached him and inquired, "You packing?"

"No."

"Get off the bike," he ordered.

Colton did so. Mr. Clean roughly searched him then attempted to shove him forward. Colton had anticipated the shove. Just prior to it, he subtly widened his stance, and planted his feet, then leaned back almost imperceptibly (lowering and strengthening his center of gravity). The result was like attempting to push a brick wall. Mr. Clean expecting Colton to stumble forward had already committed himself to stepping forward. He stumbled awkwardly into the unmoving Colton.

Colton quickly grabbed the biker's right arm at the wrist and elbow joint, with both his hands, as though trying to aid him from stumbling. He now applied firm pressure, so the biker knew he could easily break his arm if he wanted to. Smiling widely Colton said, "Easy there big guy, you almost fell. I would hate to see you break an arm or something." He immediately loosened his grip.

The biker yanked his arm away, glared at Colton and said, "Follow me. Freak, shoot him if he tries anything stupid."

Colton asked, "how would he know what that is?"

"Just shut up and walk," Mr. Clean replied.

Colton followed him inside a metal front door to the clubhouse. Freak followed close behind. The smell of spilled sour beer, combined with the tang of marijuana, filled the air. They walked down a dimly lit hall that emptied into a large room, with an oak-paneled horseshoe bar as its centerpiece.

There were about three dozen gang members gathered at side tables and the bar. Toby Keith's "I Love This Bar" was blaring on oversized speakers. Colton was led to the center point of the U-shaped bar. Everyone got quiet and the music suddenly stopped.

Chapter 40

LUCAS EXITED THE TRUCK and approached the two women. He backhanded Linda. The force of the blow knocked her to the ground.

"Ungrateful bitch," he hissed.

"What's in the bag?" Lucas asked as he hefted it from the ground and unzipped it. Linda looked at him, her eyes full of fear. Looking inside at all the cash, he whistled low and slow. "Damn—looks like you got caught with your hand in the cookie jar. Banner's going to be seriously upset with you."

"It's not what you think I ...." started Linda

"Shut up, you stupid whore. Get your butt up and head back inside, before I get really upset and shoot you."

Maggie started towards Linda to help her up, but Lucas grabbed a fistful of her hair, yanking her backwards and pulling her close to him. He wrapped his left arm around her waist while still holding her hair with his right. She struggled to free herself from his grasp, but he pulled her in closer. He leaned his face in until his cheek was pressed against hers. Maggie could smell the sour bourbon on his breath. "Your boyfriend, the cook, is coming for you soon. He actually thinks I'm going to let you go when he gets here, but it looks like we might be short one whore, so plans may have to change."

"Just let me go. I haven't done anything to you," she pleaded.

"Maybe not, but I'm going to do plenty to you," he said as he licked her neck.

Maggie increased her struggling, but Lucas held firm. "You're sick. Colton will kill you if you do anything to me."

"We'll see about that. Your little cook doesn't scare me." Lucas began dragging her back to the door they had exited just a couple minutes ago. Linda slowly stood and followed them inside.

He hauled Maggie down the hallway to a storage closet where he roughly shoved her inside along with Linda. The room was large for a closet. One of the walls was lined with metal shelves, holding cleaning supplies: trash bags, canned goods, and other items.

Maggie had her back to the shelving unit as Lucas closed and locked the door. "I'm going to start your indoctrination into our club. It's a long process before you become a full-blown bitch. Eventually, everyone gets to have you, but for now I sample the goods first." Lucas looked at her hungrily. Linda cowered in the far corner. His cell rang loudly in the confined closet. It was a call from Banner. "Hey boss what's up?"

"The cook just rode in the front gate. Freak and Jagar said he came alone and is unarmed, they're escorting him to the bar now. Ballsy bastard for sure." Whiskey said.

"How the fuck did he get here already? The son-of-a-bitch fly?"

"Don't know, but he rode to the front gate on a Harley," Banner answered.

"I'll be right there," Lucas said and punched off.

"Looks like our fun time will have to wait a few. Your boyfriend just showed up. Maybe I'll let him live awhile and make him watch. Let's get you gals back to your room."

Chapter 41

SLOAN AND JACKS TRUDGED through the underground sewer following the map to the precise spot where the red X was on their copy of the strategic assault plan. Their night vision goggles cast a bright, eerie glow in the soggy tunnel system. They were clad in black Nomak suits complete with dark tactical helmets. They both wore light body armor underneath their suits. They resembled modern ninjas.

Jacks handed his suppressed MP-5 sub machine gun to Sloan then shrugged out of his backpack. He carefully removed a pliable section of C-4 with an attached digital detonator and carefully affixed it to the sewer roof above, directly underneath the club's bar area. He activated the detonator and gave Sloan a thumbs up. He shrugged his backpack on, grabbed his gun from Sloan, then continued forward in the sewer tunnel towards the next red X that was underneath a storage closet inside the clubhouse.

"Would you look at the size of that thing," Jacks whispered to Sloan. A rat, the size of a small dog, waddled quickly away from them.

"Always the glamorous assignments for us. Shit-filled sewers with rats the size of small beagles; I should have stayed retired," replied Sloan.

"And not be able to knock some heads, and shoot to thrill, come on captain don't get too old on me," Jacks teased.

"Hey, I'm not in the extended-care facility yet, but still this place stinks—literally," Sloan complained.

"We've been in worse. Remember swimming that cesspool of a river near Cairo?"

"I tried to suppress that one from the memory banks. You're right, that was worse."

"Ok, this is it," Jacks said as he came to a stop. He repeated the same drill as at the previous spot. Once the charge was affixed, and the detonator set, they backtracked to right angle in the sewer and hunkered down.

"We have five minutes before double big-boom time. Better put on the ear protection," Sloan said.

"Yeah, I reckon so. I would hate to be deaf the rest of my life," Jacks replied.

"What?" Sloan asked.

"I said I reckon ...." Jacks stopped in mid-sentence and flipped Sloan the bird.

Sloan smiled stupidly back at him.

"I wonder if that crazy Colton is still alive, and if so, can he stay that way for five more minutes until we save the day?" Jacks asked.

"He seems like a capable guy, but a bit loosely wired to do what he is doing for sure," offered Sloan. "It's getting close, we better get on the ear protection."

They each donned their noise-cancelling headphones and waited quietly in the dark. The proverbial quiet before the storm would be a gross understatement for what awaited all of them.

Chapter 42

THE BARTENDER APPROACHED Colton from the other side of the bar and extended his hand. He resembled an aging Grateful Dead fan complete with long, gray hair, beard, an ample beer belly and, of course, the obligatory tie-dye T-shirt.

"Welcome to the Devil's Dungeon. I've heard so much about you. I'm glad we finally get to meet. I'm Ron Banner. Club president."

Colton shook the offered hand and asked, "Where's Maggie?"

"Slow down. She is fine. What you do from here on will determine if she stays that way."

Colton looked into the depths of Banner's grey eyes and held his piercing stare a moment before replying, "I can assure you the same goes for you, and your gang."

Banner started to laugh a slow, easy laugh, at first, that gradually became a full-bellied laugh. "You are every bit as cocky as Lucas said and then some. Son, you need to understand I could have you killed like that." Banner snapped his fingers for emphasis.

"You sure about that? More than a dozen of your gang members have already tried and failed miserably. You will have to forgive me if I'm not intimidated," Colton retorted.

An audible click of a gun hammer being cocked, followed by the tip of a cold barrel of a handgun, was now pressed against the back of Colton's head.

"Well, if it isn't my old buddy the cook?" Lucas said. He was holding a Colt Python 44-Magnum against the back of Colton's head.

Colton continued to stare unfazed at Banner. Several other gang members now stood up from nearby tables and bar stools, each brandishing some type of handgun, two were carrying tech-nine, fully automatic machine pistols, with extended magazines.

Colton continued to hold Banner's gaze, not even acknowledging the gun barrel against the back of his head.

Banner spoke, "Easy boys. Colton, I don't want to kill you. I really don't. Now Lucas, he really does wants to kill you, but fortunately for you, I'm the boss."

"The boss of what exactly? A group of degenerates that sell drugs to vulnerable people and prey on innocent ones?" Colton replied with disdain.

"Well now, that's quite a judgmental attitude you have. I was hoping that you may consider joining us. From what I've heard, you would make a tremendous asset to our organization here. I could use someone like you. Someone with your skills. My offer is simple. Your girlfriend walks if you agree to stay and work with us."

"Boss, what kind of bullshit is this?" Lucas complained.

"Shut up, Lucas," ordered Banner. "Obviously, Lucas and you will have to mend things up, but all in time. What do you say?"

Colton glanced at the face of his watch. It read 4:43. "No deal. Maggie is leaving with me, as well as Lucas and his sister. I suggest you agree to those terms. If you do, I can assure you no one will get hurt."

Banner started to laugh again. "Good Lord boy, you are unbelievable. No one is going to help you. The cops won't even come in here. They know better. Do you seriously think I'm going to just let you walk out the front door with your gal and Lucas?"

"No, I suppose not, but I was hoping so. I told my controller I would try to avoid making too big of a scene for a change, but, like usual, I suppose things aren't going to work out that way," Colton said.

"Your controller? Who the hell is that?" asked Banner with the first hint of irritation in his voice.

"It's a long story. The problem your guys have is they don't know the fundamentals of combat: armed or unarmed. For instance, in armed combat you never place the barrel of a gun directly against an opponent's head. It gives your victim an edge. Action is always quicker than reaction, and the fact that if Lucas pulls that trigger, he is not only going to kill me, but you as well is all the edge I need."

Before Colton finished his last word he already began to dip and spin to his left. His left hand deftly knocked the big barrel of the Colt to the right just as Lucas pulled the trigger. The booming of the huge gun temporarily deafened Colton. The errant large-caliber round struck another biker standing at the bar square in the chest, blowing him backward off the stool as though he was hit with a wrecking ball.

Colton slammed the side of Lucas' head with a short, hard, right hook. The extremely powerful punch knocked him to the floor. Lucas was fighting to not lose consciousness. Colton vaulted over the horseshoe shaped bar landing on top of Banner who was trying to draw his own Tech-nine machine pistol from underneath the bar, both men tumbled to the floor. Colton drove a vicious elbow to the side of Banner's head, rendering him unconscious. He snatched the Tech Nine from his grip.

Only a few seconds had elapsed since Colton's first move against Lucas. No one else had fired yet for fear of hitting one of their own in a crossfire, but Colton knew that edge would not last long. He rolled off Banner and onto his back. He was gazing at three bikers holding a trio of handguns aimed down at him from the front of the bar. They had hesitated to shoot while he was on top of Banner, but now he was off to the side.

Colton wished there was another way as he abhorred killing but knew he had no other choice. He depressed the trigger of the Tech Nine and sent twelve hollow-point pieces of hot lead their way. He didn't have time to take serious aim, but instead did the pray & spray method.

Several of the first rounds were low and thudded harmlessly into the dark wood of the walnut bar, causing numerous wood splinters to shower the first biker's face. He screamed as they imbedded into his cheeks, forehead, and left eye. At least Colton assumed he screamed by the large O-shape of his mouth and bulging of his eyes, as Colton was still only hearing loud ringing in his ears.

The remaining bullets climbed higher with three striking the middle biker in the right shoulder, center chest, and left shoulder. The last rounds flew harmlessly into the rear wall of the bar, as the remaining biker had wisely dropped to the floor behind the bar. The cheap gun now jammed. Colton discarded it and quickly crab-crawled to the far end of the bar towards a metal door.

Pieces of drywall and ceiling tile were now showering down on Colton from the rear wall and ceiling, as all were being shredded from a multitude of bullets, as several of the gang members were now wildly shooting.

Staying low, while quickly crawling behind the bar, Colton reached the metal door, rolled onto his back and kicked it with both feet. It crashed inward. He scampered inside and shoved the door shut behind him. He quickly engaged a heavy-duty lock just as numerous rounds impacted the other side of it.

Colton heard two low growls behind him. Slowly turning, he saw two huge dogs that resembled pit bulls on steroids complete with stud-metal collars, getting ready to attack from just a few feet away. He recalled from the strategic assault plan, that he was in Banner's office. The only exit, another door that led to an east-west hallway was blocked by both dogs. Colton was not a fan of vicious dogs. The two large canines growling at him certainly fit that category.

The dogs suddenly charged with one slightly ahead of the other. Colton spotted a small, red, fire extinguisher on the floor next to him. He grabbed it by the handle and swung it hard against the side of the lead dog's head just as it lunged upward towards his neck. The metal cylinder thudded against the dog's massive head. It yelped loudly while falling to the floor.

The second dog had settled for Colton's right boot and had clamped down on it while shaking his head vigorously back and forth. Colton could feel the long incisors penetrating the thick leather of his boot and piercing his foot. He struggled to retain his balance while he reared his left leg up, then stomped downward on its big head. It yelped and released its hold. Colton now leapt over the dogs and ran to the other door. Yanking it open, he jumped into the hallway, and slammed it shut just as both of the animals flung themselves against it.

Colton, perspiring and breathing heavily, focused on calming himself down. *Come on Sloan and Jacks, where are you?* he thought.

He was answered promptly as two powerful explosions knocked him to the floor. The few lights on in the hallway blinked out and alarms started ringing. *Thank God,* he thought. Sloan and Jacks were in.

Chapter 43

D.P.D. DETECTIVE SMITH looked back at Ricco flying the chopper. They had dropped off Colton, Jacks, and Sloan a half-hour earlier on the outskirts of the city and were currently inbound to the Devil Dungeon's compound. Dirk was wondering if he had gone completely insane. He was less than a year from retirement, and now he was risking it all by teaming up with a group of rouge mercenaries about to assault the most heavily guarded enemy fortress in the city of Detroit.

The truth was he had never felt better. His mind felt clearer than it had in years. Ricco gave Dirk the thumbs up and spoke into his headset. "It's time to lock & load detective; we have lots of ammo, so spread the lead!"

Ricco shoved the chopper into a sharp descent. Dirk was strapped in a seat behind the massive machine gun with protective metal shield. Wearing night vision goggles he could easily see the compound looming ahead.

"Just keep us out of those power lines, and I'll be happy," Dirk replied.

Ricco glanced at his watch and saw it was 4:45 am. They were right on time, as they were closing in on the compound, all of its bright, exterior lights suddenly blinked out. Although the explosions in the sewer were not visible, Ricco knew they had occurred. Jacks and Sloan did their job.

Ricco spotted a few perimeter guards walking the interior fence line. He dove the chopper towards them. Although the chopper lights were off, it was still very loud. No doubt the guys below were confused at hearing a helicopter practically on top of them but not being able to see much except a dark shadow.

Ricco hovered, then angled Dirk's open side towards the guards. Dirk smiled as he took aim and depressed the trigger on the big gun. "Good morning, assholes," he yelled while depressing the trigger on the huge gun. The rounds impacted the gravel near the perimeter guard's feet, showering them with gravel and dirt. They turned and scrambled for any cover they could find.

"The bees are starting to leave their hive. Light those bastards up, Dirk," Ricco said into the headset, while pointing at the nearby barracks.

Dirk swiveled the gun to his right and saw several armed gang members running from the smaller barracks towards the main clubhouse. He fired several rounds near the first biker who was carrying a shotgun. The biker foolishly fired a round at the chopper. *So much for being nice* thought Dirk as he took careful aim and fired again. The biker immediately crumbled to the ground.

The remaining bikers ran back towards the barracks, with a trail of red tracer bullets tearing up the ground at their heels. Dirk was trying to honor Colton's request of shooting to kill only if fired upon.

Small arms fire erupted from several windows of the barracks. One round clanged off the shield inches from Dirk's face. "Ok, that was way too close. No more Mr. Nice guy." Dirk now sprayed the entire side of the barracks windows with over 1500 rounds. Glass and concrete block were torn up as though being eaten by a swarm of locusts with steel teeth.

"Oh shit," exclaimed Ricco, as he saw a gang member emerge from the guard shack on the roof of the main warehouse 100 yards away. He was carrying what appeared to be a rocket propelled grenade launcher on his shoulder. He quickly kneeled, flipped Ricco the bird, and depressed the trigger.

Ricco figured the gang would be heavily armored, but never suspected they would have R.P.G.'s. He immediately realized that they were in deep shit, as at 100 yards the biker couldn't possibly miss, even if they only appeared as a shadow to him.

"Incoming, hang on!" Ricco screamed to Dirk, while he quickly pushed the chopper downward hoping not to take a direct hit to the cockpit. The grenade streaked towards them with white smoke trailing behind it like a small comet. It sailed over the cockpit, but struck the spinning rotors, blowing them apart.

The chopper nose-dived. Luckily it was only about a hundred feet off the ground when struck. It crashed face first into the gravel lot, then fell backwards onto its skids. The bubble windshield was shattered. Ricco was dazed and bleeding badly from a gash over his forehead. He surely would have died had they been any higher. Dirk would be extremely sore later but was fine for now. "What the hell happened?" He asked Ricco.

"Some jackass on the roof shot us with an RPG. Damn these guys are ready for war," muttered Ricco.

"Ricco, you're bleeding bad. Are you ok?"

"I'm good. Just get unbuckled, and get the hell out of here, we're sitting ducks, and we still need to keep those guys contained to the barracks. I'll stop the bleeding later."

They quickly unstrapped themselves and jumped out of the wrecked chopper.

The biker, who shot down the chopper, was now trying to shoot them with a handgun but was too far away to be effective. However, he was easily in rifle range. Ricco pulled up his AR-15 and shot the biker on the roof twice in the chest. He tumbled forward unceremoniously to the gravel lot below. "That was for wrecking my bird, asshole."

"Nice shooting," said Dirk. He sought cover behind a nearby pick-up truck and checked his .45 Smith & Wesson pistol, as well as a Remington, police-special, shotgun that was chambered with 5 rounds and slung to his back. He unslung the shotgun and rested the barrel of the shotgun across the hood of the truck. Two bikers rounded the far-left corner of the barracks at a fast trot each carrying their own shotguns.

Ricco, who was positioned behind a nearby Ford yelled, "Stop! Drop your weapons." Both glanced his way and raised their shotguns. "Bad decision," Ricco mumbled to himself before shooting the lead one twice in the chest. The force of the rounds knocked him backwards off his feet. Ricco stitched a trio of rounds in a tight pattern in the other guys chest as well before either had a chance to fire. Both were dead before hitting the ground. "Sorry, Colton."

Several rounds suddenly impacted the truck Dirk was concealed behind.

Ricco saw the muzzle-flash of the offending machine gun and heard the distinctive sound that only a Russian AK-47 makes. A decent weapon in the hands of a trained shooter for sure.

Ricco leaned away from his cover and let loose a folly towards the location of the muzzle flash. Several more rounds now struck the corner of the car inches from his face. "Damn! That guy can shoot," he hissed to himself as he ducked behind the van again.

Dirk moved to the rear of the pickup, then belly crawled across the opposite side. He could now see Ricco about twenty-five feet to his left behind the Ford. There were at least two shooters now, directing multiple rounds at both the truck and the car. They appeared to be hunkered down behind a junky, rusted-out Cadillac, some seventy or so feet away near the barracks.

Dirk hand signaled Ricco that he was going to run to the front of another truck, parked between the shooters and them, and engage them from there.

Ricco nodded his approval. Ricco let loose with another volley to distract the shooter while Dirk scrambled to the front of the other truck.

As soon as the shooting paused, Dirk popped up over the hood and let loose with three rounds from his .45. As he did so, Ricco lobbed two smoke grenades between them. Heavy gray/black smoke began spewing from the canisters, obscuring their field of vision.

Ricco signaled for Dirk to flank the shooter's left side, while he did the right. They both sprinted to opposite sides of the Cadillac, about twenty yards apart from each other. They now saw the bikers, who made the amateurish mistake of reloading at the same time. They immediately dropped their empty weapons and raised their hands.

"You bastards have Colton to thank for me not shooting you dead right now," grumbled Ricco. "Cuff 'em up. I'll gladly shoot either of them if they resist," Ricco said to Dirk, who moved in and secured both with plastic flex-cuffs behind their backs with the efficiency of someone who had done so hundreds of times. He then removed a roll of duct tape from his jacket pocket and taped their legs together. Once that task was complete, Dirk placed an extra piece of tape over each biker's mouth.

Ricco hunkered down next to him and said, "Put some of that tape over my head wound. The blood keeps running in my eyes." Dirk wiped off Ricco's forehead with his sleeve, then taped it up with duct tape. The bleeding slowed considerably.

"Thanks. Now, let's get back behind our original cover and make sure no one else makes it out of that barracks. I'm sure Colton and company have their hands full inside," Ricco said.

"I sure wish we hadn't left those Motorolas behind. Would have been nice to have some radio contact with each other," Ricco said. "Damn Jacks. He always forgets something. At least it wasn't the guns this time."

Dirk glanced at his watch; it read 0451. Colton had instructed them to hold in place until 0457 then get the hell out, if he wasn't at the roof for extraction by then. Of course, without a functioning chopper, that was not an option now.

"We got five more minutes before Colton said to split, no matter what," Dirk said to Ricco who nodded his agreement.

"We will, but five minutes is a long time."

They hurried through the smoke and took up their positions once again behind the vehicles.

Chapter 44

COLTON HEARD MUFFLED shooting from the intersecting hallway. Despite not having night vision goggles, he could see fine. This was an attribute he had since birth. An optometrist once explained to him that he had more rods or cones, Colton couldn't quite remember which, than the majority of the population. In fact, he was in the top ½ %. This enabled him to see exceptionally well in low light. His ears were still ringing loudly but some of his hearing was returning.

Colton did a quick peek around the corner and saw two bodies of gang members sprawled in the hallway. He stepped cautiously into it walking towards them just as a shadowy figure stepped out of a nearby doorway.

Colton immediately put up his hands and whispered, "Don't shoot, it's me."

"You're damn lucky I didn't have too much caffeine this morning," Sloan replied while stepping over the bodies and approaching Colton. "Sorry, but they left me no choice," Sloan lied.

"Is Maggie safe?" Colton asked.

"Yes, Jacks is taking her and the girl out now," Sloan said while withdrawing a .40 caliber Glock and handing it to Colton, along with a spare magazine. "I'm glad to see you're still alive."

Colton took the weapon and spare magazine. "You too. Now let's go get Lucas and get out of here," Colton said while leading Sloan back to Banner's office door. "I left him dazed, but he is probably coming around now unless the explosion killed him. Get ready. There are two mean ass dogs on the other side of this door, and a whole bunch of pissed off bikers on the other side of the door after that," Colton warned.

"Sounds like a fun time," Sloan replied with a grin as Colton yanked open the door.

Colton flattened himself against the wall. Sloan was standing with his MP-5 at the ready—waist high. The dogs charged low and fast. Sloan dispatched both dogs with single shots to their heads. Colton leapt over the dogs and walked quickly to the other door with Sloan following. He looked at Sloan, counted down from three to one on his fingers, then yanked open the door.

Colton darted left and low into the room, hunkering down behind the bar. He had the handgun held in front of him in a two-hand, police-style grip. Sloan scrambled forward following him into the room staying in a low crouch and went right. They popped up quickly and scanned the darkened room. There were several bodies lying about, undoubtedly knocked unconscious by the blast. They saw no active threats.

Colton vaulted the counter and found Lucas groggily trying to stand just on the other side. He placed the gun in his waistband, then pushed him backwards a few feet into the gaping hole in the floor. Lucas landed very unceremoniously on his butt, in the sewer ten feet below. Colton jumped down landing next to him.

Sloan was about to join him when he heard a booming noise and felt as though he was hit with a baseball bat to his upper thigh. He fell to his knees then turned behind him to address the threat. Whiskey Banner was standing several feet away holding the large Colt Python that Lucas had earlier.

Colton heard the shot, glanced upwards and saw Sloan fall backwards away from the hole. Colton leapt upwards, grabbing the floor's jagged edge, and began to pull himself up when he was suddenly yanked back down. His head slammed into the sewer's hard concrete floor. A few inches of water that had accumulated on the bottom was just enough of a cushion to prevent him from being knocked unconscious, but as it was, he was badly dazed.

Lucas straddled him and punched him hard with a straight, right jab. Colton felt his nose break for the second time in his life. Lucas followed up with a hard left-hook that impacted the side of Colton's head. Colton fought to stay conscious. He attempted to deliver a straight jab to Lucas' throat, but the punch was slow, and Lucas easily twisted away from it.

Lucas laughed and said, "Not so tough now, are you? I've been waiting for this moment a long time." He grabbed Colton on either side of his shoulders and leaned back until Colton's head and torso were several inches from the floor. "Time to take you out of the equation, cook." He violently shoved Colton's shoulders back down. His head impacted the hard cement a second time with a sickening thud. This time Colton lost the battle for consciousness.

Chapter 45

DIRK AND RICCO WERE focused on the barracks ahead of them, as nothing was behind them except for the rear fence, and a couple more parked vehicles. The compound resembled the war zone it had become; their crashed helicopter was nearby, smoke obscured their field of vision as it still spewed from the canisters; buildings and vehicles had battle scars from numerous bullets impacting them.

Ricco spotted a shadowy figure running towards them from the far corner of the barracks. He attempted to track the figure with his rifle, but the smoke made it difficult. He thought he saw the partially obscured gang member hurl something towards him. The soup-can-sized object rolled underneath the Ford he was hunkered behind.

Dirk made a similar observation, but of a different gang member, who had come from the opposite corner of the barracks.

Ricco and Dirk yelled at the same time, "Grenades!"

The dual concussive blasts propelled both the car and pickup skyward a couple feet before each settled back to the ground. The vehicles remained mostly intact, minus their window glass which was blown out. A hood was blown skyward off one of the vehicles. Fortunately, both vehicle's fuel tanks were nearly empty, and the grenades had settled closer to the engine blocks than the gas tanks. Secondary blasts would have surely killed them. The engine blocks absorbed most of the shrapnel and blast, but not all of it.

Dirk dove away from the truck just prior to the explosion, laying on his back in the gravel, barely conscious. He slowly blinked open his eyes. His entire body throbbed. He felt like he went 12 rounds with several professional boxers. Blood leaked from his ears and nose. The ringing in his ears was deafening. He groggily scanned the area for his shotgun, but it was nowhere in sight. The hood of the pickup clanged to the ground three feet away from him, like part of a meteor.

He struggled mightily to a standing position looking for Ricco, but instead saw a well-muscled gang member, that he thought resembled Mr. Clean from the commercials, striding through the smoke towards him. He was carrying a shotgun, and upon reaching him jabbed the butt of the shotgun hard into his chest knocking him off his feet. Dirk coughed and groaned, once again he was on his back on the gravel.

"I don't know who you are, but you made a real big mistake coming here and fucking with us," the biker said while racking a round into the 12 gauge.

Dirk was shocked that he could hear him talk with the ringing in his ears like dueling air-raid sirens. He was too old for this shit; every tendon, muscle, and fiber of his being hurt like hell. He pretty much figured this mission was a suicide mission anyways.

Truth was Dirk wasn't overly happy with his life. Three failed marriages, three kids—two that didn't speak to him—and in debt beyond belief was what the golden years of retirement had in store for him, but he did have a glimpse of what sobriety did for him. He hadn't felt so clear headed as he did in the past twelve hours. Maybe things could get better for him, but his future didn't look to promising at the moment.

"Time to die old man," Mr. Clean said while lowering the shotgun barrel towards him.

In the end, when he later had time to think about it, it was the old man comment that did it. Dirk wasn't about to die at the hands of this clown without a fight. He spied a small matte-black handle of what presumably was a knife protruding from the biker's boot top. It was almost within his reach. Dirk purposely turned his head the opposite way as though giving in to the inevitable, but not wanting to see it coming, hoping the biker would take the bait.

"That's right, grandpa, look away. I wouldn't want to see it coming either," Mr. Clean jeered.

Dirk smiled inwardly, the diversion worked. He scooped up some dirt and gravel in his right hand and suddenly flung it into the biker's face while rolling towards him. The biker fired blindly before the barrel was on the now moving target. Numerous buckshot pellets struck the ground where Dirk had just been. He continued the roll into the gang member's legs, knocking him off balance while smoothly snatching the knife from the boot. He buried the four-inch blade to the hilt into Mr. Clean's upper thigh.

The biker howled in pain. He desperately tried to rack another round into the chamber, but Dirk had clamped both hands on the barrel. He yanked it violently down wrenching it free of the wounded biker's grasp. Dirk half sat up while swinging the gun by the barrel, like a baseball bat, hoping to hit a home-run. The wooden stock smacked squarely against the side of the biker's face. His orbital socket cracked, and his jaw dislodged as did a few teeth.

Dirk tossed the gun behind him and grabbed the biker's legs, forcing him to the ground onto his back. Panting heavily, with exertion and pain, Dirk crawled on top of him pulling out the dagger that was still imbedded in the guy's thigh. Dirk now held it against his throat. The biker shut his eyes.

"That's ok, I wouldn't want to see it coming either," Dirk mimicked the biker's words from a few second ago. "How's it feel to get your ass kicked by a grandpa?" Dirk dismounted the dazed biker, spun him roughly over and flex cuffed his hands.

Dirk gazed about and spotted Ricco standing just a few feet away. "Are you done messing around? That was sloppy as all hell. It took way too long; you cops sure need some serious instruction on hand-to-hand combat," Ricco said.

"Yeah, well, thanks for all the help," Dirk replied sarcastically between breaths. He slowly stood up and brushed himself off.

Sirens could be heard approaching in the distance.

Dirk glanced at his watch. "It's time to go. Hopefully, the guys are no longer inside."

"Damn already. I was just starting to enjoy myself," Ricco said. His left arm hung oddly at his side, and his bandaged head was again bleeding freely. His face was pocketed with small gravel and shrapnel, but he was grinning despite it all.

"You special ops guys are a few marbles short of a bag."

With that said they both limped and gimped towards the rear fence. The remaining smoke began to dissipate in the light breeze, like incense at a funeral.

Chapter 46

THE THREE WOMEN HUDDLED together in the center of the room after the explosion.

"It's Colton, I know it is," exclaimed Allison.

"I hope he brought along some help, because no way one guy is going to get us out of here," replied Linda.

There was a tentative knock at the door. "Allison, Maggie?" inquired a stranger's voice. "Are you in there?"

"We are," replied Maggie.

"I'm a friend of Colton's. Stand away from the door; I'm going to shoot the lock."

A few seconds later they were standing in the darkened hallway with Jacks who had explained their getaway plan. Linda shook her head and said, " I'm staying. If you guys take Lucas with you, I will be fine. I have unfinished business here."

"Ok. That's your choice. Maggie, Allison we need to scoot. Follow me and stay low." The girls quickly hugged Linda then followed Jacks who crept forward in a crouch down the hallway sweeping his MP-5 from side to side ready to engage any threats.

A few minutes later Jacks pushed the manhole cover up a few inches and carefully peered out. All looked good. They were on the other side of the fence now. The semi-tractor, minus the hogs and trailer, idled across the street. Jacks climbed out of the sewer, then helped Maggie and Allison.

"Hurry up, come this way," he urged. He led them to the semi-tractor and slapped his hand against the side of the passenger door. It swung open. The driver was leaning across the seats holding a sawed-off shotgun.

"Easy my friend, it's me," said Jacks.

"I was getting worried; I heard a lot of gunshots," said the pig farmer.

"Yeah, well it's not over yet, but get these two ladies to the safe house, and stay there until you hear from us."

"Will do."

Jacks helped Allison into the cab then turned to help Maggie up. She hugged him tightly. "Thank you and be careful. Please don't let anything happen to Colton," she pleaded.

"Always am and will do Ma'am," Jacks replied. *Damn good-looking gal. That Colton is a lucky dog. If the guy doesn't make it out, I may have to console the poor lass myself, Jacks* thought as he jogged back to the sewer entrance.

• • • •

RICARDO CURSED HIMSELF for his weakness as he yanked open his bottom desk drawer and rummaged through some papers until he found the half-empty pack of cigarettes. It was a vice he was not proud of even though he rarely indulged. He felt guilty about the weakness. "Screw it," he said aloud as he shook one out and placed it between his lips. His third in as many hours.

He found the metal lighter, flicked up a tiny flame to life, lit the end, and inhaled deeply. The warm smoke comforted him as he held it inside his lungs a moment then slowly released it through his nose. He took another long slow drag. The thin paper wrapping receded quickly with the tip glowing brightly.

He abruptly stood and walked to the window, cranked it open an inch, and dropped the half-smoked cigarette to the piazza below. Damn it if he didn't feel helpless at times like this. He started to pace his office again, furtively glancing at his satellite phone atop his desk awaiting Colton's call.

Chapter 47

SLOAN PLACED A THREE-round burst from his MP-5 into Whiskey Banner's chest before Banner could fire again. Several more gang members were climbing up from the debris caused by the earlier blast and starting to get their bearings. Sloan grabbed a flash-bang grenade from his side pocket and tossed it their way and followed it up with a smoke cannister. The ear-splitting blast, along with blinding light and thick smoke, would disorient them all over again.

Sloan ignored the chunk out of his upper thigh and dove into the hole in the floor just as the flash bang went off. He fell onto Lucas, who was straddling an unconscious Colton, then rolled a few feet away. He quickly knelt and leveled the MP-5 at Lucas, trying to ignore the burning pain in his thigh. "Move a muscle and you die in this sewer," Sloan said through clenched teeth.

Lucas looked at him oddly. "What is your greatest fear?" he asked in a haunting voice.

"I'm not afraid of anything on this earth," Sloan replied.

"I didn't limit my question to this earth, Mr. Sloan."

Sloan felt a sudden chill from deep within him. "How do you know my name. Have we met before?" inquired Sloan.

"You're not talking with Lucas, I'm merely using him to communicate. I am Botis."

"Yeah, right. Enough of this bullshit. Turn around and raise your hands," ordered Sloan.

Lucas ignored him. "I recall a young Sloan who was accidentally locked in a basement cellar. When his Momma finally found him, he had pissed his pants. It was because of all the rats that came out while he waited for his Mommy to find him. Isn't that right? So, Captain Sloan, are you still afraid of rats?"

Sloan was unnerved. How in the hell did this guy know about that? It was impossible. He never told anyone. Sloan sensed movement behind him, very close movement. He turned to briefly look; there were dozens of large sewer rats, the size of small dogs. Several jumped on him.

Sloan screamed falling backwards while roughly brushing away the rats that were all over him. He was in full panic mode, thrashing and splashing around in the watery sewer. He felt like he did as that helpless child many years ago.

"Leave him be!" Colton's strong voice commanded.

The rats immediately retreated, scurrying away as though fleeing for their lives.

"Jesus," Sloan said while shakily standing. Colton was now standing; there was no sign of Lucas.

"Not even close, but I'll have to do for now," Colton replied while rubbing the back of his head.

Sloan looked incredulously at Colton. "How did you do that?"

"Do what?"

"Get rats to obey you?"

"Rats, is that what you were flailing your arms all around for and screaming like a girl? There weren't any rats. Botis is good at using your fears against you. You're injured," Colton said noticing Sloan's bloody pant leg for the first time.

"Well, aren't you a regular Sherlock Holmes!"

Sloan reached into his fanny pack and removed some quick-clot gauze and pressed it against his thigh. Tossing Colton a roll of duct tape, he instructed him to circle his leg twice while he held the gauze in place. Sloan retrieved a hypodermic needle from another pocket and injected morphine into the same thigh.

"Ok. I'm good to go. You can tell me who the hell Botis is later, but there were rats. lots of damn big ass rats!"

"Trust me, things will probably get worse when we find him again."

"Wonderful. I can hardly wait."

Two gunshots echoed from farther down the sewer. Colton began to sprint that way. Sloan, now limping, quickly fell behind. Colton saw two figures wrestling ahead in the darkened sewer. It was Lucas and Jacks. Lucas had Jacks in a rear neck hold. Jacks was trying to free himself when Lucas suddenly jerked his neck violently upwards. The cracking of bones was audible. Jacks body went limp. Lucas dropped him to the sewer's floor.

Sloan who had now caught up to Colton, bellowed, "No!" then shoved Colton aside and brought up his MP-5. Colton pushed the barrel away just as Sloan squeezed off a three-round burst.

"I need him alive," Colton said, then sprinted forward as Lucas was trying to wrest free Jacks own MP-5 from his now lifeless body.

Colton leapt forward and delivered a punishing right cross to the side of Lucas' head. Lucas stumbled sideways falling to his knees. Colton heard running, and turned, just as Sloan lowered his shoulder into Colton's side. Colton tumbled sideways rolling over in the sewer. He ended up on his hands and knees and saw Sloan just a few feet away pointing a .45 caliber pistol at Lucas.

"Sloan don't do it. You don't understand why, but believe me, it will be much worse if he dies!"

Sloan was breathing ragged breaths. "Screw that this guy is a piece of shit. He killed Jacks. He dies now, and his body stays in this stinking sewer where it belongs!" Sloan yelled, his voice filled with fury.

"Sloan, not everyone deserves to die at your hands, no matter what they have done. Let him live, trust me on this one," Colton pleaded. "Stick to the plan," Colton urged. I know he was a good friend and didn't deserve to die like this, but killing Lucas is not the solution. There is more going on here than you know. I promise you Lucas will pay for murdering your friend. Please trust me. I'm begging you."

Sloan kept his handgun level. "Move an inch, say one thing, and I swear I'll kill you. Not one word!" he said to Lucas.

Sloan nodded to Colton, then viciously kicked Lucas in the ribs, knocking him against the sewer wall. Sloan smiled at the sound of several ribs cracking. "That was for Jacks." Sloan removed a small gun from his fanny pack, pointed it at his neck and pulled the trigger. A small dart struck Lucas in the neck. Lucas reached for it but collapsed unconscious to the sewer floor before he could remove it.

"Thank you, Sloan," Colton said with sincerity.

Chapter 48

LUCAS WOKE SLOWLY, and groggily, as the powerful sedative wore off. He was laying on his back on a marble altar. He noticed that his hands were cuffed together with his arms stretched backwards behind his head. The handcuffs were attached to a thick metal chain that ran to the floor. His ankles were similarly bound. Another heavy chain completely wound around his torso and the altar. It was secured with a large padlock.

Moonlight filtered in from the early morning sky through stained-glass windows high above. Numerous candles were lit that added additional illumination to the interior. Lucas glanced to his left and saw a wooden crucifix mounted high on the wall, with a statue of the Blessed Mother below it. He groaned not so much from his pain, but from the slow realization he was in enemy territory—a church!

"Welcome Lucas; I am Father Hunt. I am here to help you."

Lucas glanced to his right; a tall priest clad in traditional black with white collar stood before him. Colton stood a few feet behind him, arms crossed gazing wearily at Justin. Sloan stood next to Colton with the hardened gaze of a trained professional killer.

"Help me. Seriously. I'm bound as though I'm the Incredible Hulk! This doesn't look like the start to helping someone. Besides, I don't need your help. I hate priests. Where am I?" Lucas replied while tugging at his restraints. The chains rattled securely against the altar.

"You are in a recently shuttered Catholic Church not too far from your clubhouse, but that should be the least of your concerns now. Where you go when your life departs you is what should be of your greatest concern. Believe it or not, all of us want to help you but the restraints, unfortunately, are necessary," Father Hunt replied.

"Save your religious babble. It's garbage to me. Your God is not mine," Lucas hissed.

"Ahh, but there you are wrong, Mr. Sledge. My God is your God as there is only one God. As difficult as this may be to believe, he has enough mercy and grace for all, even you."

"This is bullshit. Let me kill this bastard slowly," Sloan whispered not so quietly to Colton and took a step forward. Colton gently placed a hand on his shoulder.

"Give it time, Sloan. Give it time," Colton urged.

Suddenly, Lucas went rigid as though jolted by electricity. His pupils rolled upwards so only the whites of his eye were visible. He began to tremble violently. White foam seeped from the corners of his mouth, and blood leaked from his nose.

"Kill me, asshole. Kill me!" He hissed at Sloan in the same haunting voice Sloan recognized from the sewer.

Sloan looked at Colton then back to Lucas.

"Come on you piece of shit. Kill me like I killed your pathetic friend. I snapped his scrawny neck like a farmer does a chicken."

Sloan let out a low growl then shrugged off Colton's grasp and ran towards Lucas, wrapping both his hands around his neck and began choking him. "I'll gladly kill you!" Sloan shouted at him filled with rage.

Lucas hoarsely encouraged him, "Do it. Do it."

Colton ran to the altar attempting to pull Sloan off Lucas while Father Hunt chanted an unintelligible prayer nearby. Sloan continued to choke Lucas whose blank eyes were now bulging. Colton pleaded with Sloan to stop but was ignored. Colton was about to subdue Sloan when they were suddenly pelted with raindrops.

Colton was momentarily confused as it couldn't be raining inside the church. He glanced behind him and saw Father Hunt liberally sprinkling holy water on all three of them.

Lucas screamed a horrific, mind-numbing, "No!" His body actually sizzled, and steam rose from it as the water pelted him.

Sloan quickly released his grasp on Lucas and stepped backwards. "What the bloody hell," he mumbled.

A coolness suddenly enveloped the room, not unlike walking into an upright freezer. Colton stepped between Lucas and Sloan. "Noooooo—stay away from me, disciple of Christ," Lucas yelled.

Colton stopped as Lucas snapped the chain on the cuffs that restrained his wrists as though they were plastic. He then grabbed the chain around his chest and pulled hard. His face reddening with exertion, a link snapped apart. Lucas was almost free. Sitting upright now, he attempted to grab the cuffs around his feet when Colton lunged forward grabbing him by the shoulders. He forced him back on the marble slab of the altar.

Father Hunt continued chanting and now was holding a small, metal censer attached to a chain that was emitting incense. He quickly circled the altar while grey smoke trailed from the cannister behind him filling the church with its strong scent.

Sloan ran to the other side of the altar and assisted Colton in restraining Lucas. His rigid body suddenly went slack. His eyes were no longer rolled upwards, and his mouth no longer foamed. Lucas started to giggle softly at first, but it soon became a full-bellied laugh. Sloan glanced perplexedly at Colton. After a couple minutes the laughing finally subsided.

Father Hunt lowered the incense canister and approached the altar. He placed a hand on Sloan's shoulder, "you cannot beat this foe with brute force alone."

"Finally, you speak the truth, preacher. None of you will ever defeat me. I have lived a hundred lives and will live a hundred more."

"In the name of the Lord Jesus Christ, I order you to leave this man!" Father Hunt said while making the sign of the cross over Lucas.

"Who are you to order me? I am more powerful than you will ever be. You are too weak to even save half of your own congregation from the depths of my ruler's prisons. How can you possibly save Lucas?"

"Don't you dare speak of my congregation. You cannot possibly know where their souls will reside. Only the Holy Father knows that!"

"Enough of this!" Lucas shouted, then suddenly shoved Colton and Sloan away. Both flew backwards as though struck by hurricane-force winds. Sloan crashed into the wall under the giant crucifix with a thud, his body partially breaking through the plaster. Colton slammed into the first row of pews twenty feet away, the impact of his body knocking a whole section loose, with him tumbling over them and landing in the second row. Lucas quickly sat up snapping the chains around his ankles as though they were made of string. He pushed himself off the altar now and stood nose to nose with the priest.

"I am not afraid of you," Father Hunt said, despite his visible trembling.

"Ah, but I think you are." Lucas backhanded the priest who buckled to the floor. "Denounce your faith, father."

Father Hunt glowered at Lucas as a trickle of blood leaked from the corner of his mouth. "Never!"

Lucas reared back his fist to strike the priest again.

"Leave him alone, Botis; I know Lucas is only your vessel," ordered Colton. "You may be stronger than I, but you are not more powerful than who I serve, for I am a disciple of Christ—a holy warrior for him and protector of the faith." Colton was surprised at the words he had just spoken and with the authority he did.

"So, you finally acknowledge who you are. "What has the once mighty Samson to do with this. Does he still think more of his women than he does his Lord?"

"You apparently don't know me as well as you think you do. It's time to send you to the chasm once and for all," countered Colton who once again was surprised at his words. He felt surreal as though he was no longer in control of his speech.

Botis laughed; a haunting laugh that echoed about the church.

"Go ahead and laugh. You are defeated. You cannot possibly win in this environment, no matter how powerful you may be to the unfaithful, you are weakened here," Colton said.

"Weakened, really. The fine father's ancient recitations, incense, and holy water did little good. I am like some bacteria that your ignorant doctors cannot defeat. I've built a resistance to your usual tricks."

"Well then, I suppose I will have to go the route of the unusual. Father Hunt, the rosary please," stated Colton.

Father Hunt shakily stood. He reached into his front pocket and withdrew the prayer beads.

"A simple rosary. You think that will help you? You Catholics are such fools," taunted Botis.

"This is no simple rosary. It is the Rosary given to St. Dominic by our Blessed Mother during an apparition in 1214. I brought the relic with me from the Vatican vault." Before Colton's words were finished, he moved quickly forward looping the rosary over Lucas's head.

The translucent ivory beads and golden cross seemed to weigh hundreds of pounds, as Lucas groaned and collapsed to his knees before sagging forward onto the floor where he writhed in pain. Sweat dripped from his brow onto the tiled floor despite the cool air.

Father Hunt stood over him, arms extended in prayer chanting incomprehensible words.

Lucas began to convulse. The church began to vibrate as though a low-level earthquake was occurring. His prostrate body began to levitate from the floor.

Sloan had finally extricated himself from the wall and walked unsteadily towards Colton and the priest. He muttered, "Jesus," at the spectacle.

"Yes, I would certainly agree he is here," Colton said in an awestruck hushed tone.

"Leave this man! In the name of our savior give him peace!" Father Hunt implored, his arms still outstretched over the prostrate levitating body of Lucas.

"Samson stop this priest, and I will make you king of this world, "implored Botis. Lucas' body was contorting in obvious pain.

Colton looked at Lucas and asked, "What good is it to gain this world and lose any chance at a heavenly reward. You are a corrupt being destined for Hell. I prefer to set my sights on eternity and to reside above. My faith may not be as strong as it could be, but it is beyond your temptations."

The steady low-level rumbling of the church continued. Fissures began to appear in the walls, pews rattled & cracked. Pieces of stained glass rained down upon them as the windows high above shattered. Sloan gazed all about, then frantically made the sign of the cross for the first time in years. "If this is him weakened than God help us," he muttered.

• • • •

"YOU ARE A FOOL. KILL the priest, stop him!"

"I am but a simple man," Colton replied.

"Ah, but there you are wrong; you have Samson's spirit. You are but a vessel as well. You are no more Colton Bishop than I am Lucas Sledge," groaned Botis who was almost in too much agony to speak intelligibly.

"You don't know anything about who I am?" Colton retorted.

"Oh, but I do."

The old church bells that hadn't rang in over a year began to clang violently. Hundreds of bats suddenly appeared and swooped all about them.

Sloan swore and swatted then away.

Father Hunt interrupted, "enough babble. Be gone from this man."

"No! I am Botis. I must kill your earthly shepherd; remove this rosary from me!"

"You will do no such thing. You know what you have to do. Colton has left you an option, in a semi-truck parked just outside these walls, as opposed to banishment to the abyss. I suggest you leave this man while you have the chance," Father Hunt explained.

"The choice is yours, Botis, but you had better make it quick; otherwise you and Lucas both die here," Colton added.

Lucas clenched his fist and Botis screamed, "Damn you all to Hell." The scream was filled with the terror of thousands of dead, condemned souls. It was the most inhumane scream any of them had ever heard.

The bells suddenly stopped clanging, the church quit shaking, and the bats flew out of the broken windows, as Lucas crumpled to the church floor with a heavy final thud.

Chapter 49

"WHAT JUST HAPPENED here?" asked Sloan in an incredulous tone.

Lucas was still prostrate on the floor, limp as a rag doll. Father Hunt was calmly extinguishing the candles.

"You just witnessed a seldom used practice in this country—an exorcism," replied Colton.

"Is he dead?" Sloan asked.

"No. It usually takes them a few minutes to come around afterwards," Colton offered.

"You've witnessed this before?" Sloan inquired with awe.

"Yeah. Several times."

"So, can I kill the bastard now?"

Colton laughed. "No, Sloan. You can't. Killing him won't bring Jacks back. Besides, the one most responsible is no longer residing in him. Now we call the police."

"Huh. Well that sucks, cause I still want to kill him."

"I know, but I think you'll find he's different now. He may still have something positive to contribute to society."

"Well, that would truly be a miracle if this piece of crap has anything positive to contribute besides being protein for worms."

Colton laughed again.

Father Hunt approached them looking exhausted. "Well, this has been a most interesting evening."

"It surely has father. Sorry you were dragged into this, but exorcisms are not my specialty," explained Colton.

"Well you certainly appear to have a specialty. I don't suppose you can share with us exactly who, or what, you are?" the priest inquired.

Colton stood in silence for a long moment before Sloan interjected, "I don't know my Bible too well but are you really Samson?" he asked with a wry smile.

Colton laughed again. "Hardly. No, I'm just a guy like you that walks the same earth you walk but sometimes am assisted by things that I can't comprehend."

"You have been called to your path, son, and you follow in faith; that much is evident. Sometimes I suppose it is best to simply live, and let live, and save the questions for later when we meet our dear maker," offered the priest.

"I suppose so father, but I can't help to wonder, why should such tasks be assigned to me. I'm no one special. There are far better Christians than I."

"Christians aren't perfect, just forgiven. Remember, the original apostles were far from perfect. Besides, sometimes when we fight pure evil one has to get a bit dirty, and you appear comfortable in the mud, my son. No offense, just an observation."

"None taken father," Colton replied.

"Huh, that's profound. I'm going to ponder that over a few beers later. If you don't need me anymore, I'm going to go take care of Jacks' body. I'm sure going to miss that kid. He was a great soldier," Sloan added.

"I'm really sorry about Jacks. We will make sure that anything his family needs is taken care of," Colton said.

"I appreciate that, but who exactly is we? Sloan asked looking steadily at Colton, "Yeah, I know you can't tell me."

"Jacks died for a very noble cause today. I'm certain he will be rewarded for that," Colton offered.

"Most assuredly," offered Father Hunt.

"Thanks guys. I appreciate it. I need to run now. Ricco and I need medical attention of a discreet nature. Besides, the longer I'm here, the more chance of the cops finding us, and I don't need that complication. Anyhow, take care, and if you ever need help again don't freaking call me," Sloan said with a slow smile. They shook hands and Sloan limped out of the church.

The pig farmer was parked just outside the old church as instructed. He wondered what could possibly be happening inside as he sat in his cab listening to a radio talk show touting the merits of fish oil. The sun was slowly rising on a new day. The first of its warm shafts of light began to penetrate his truck's window. His cargo of sixty-six hogs was mostly quiet, except for an occasional grunt.

The farmer reached for his Styrofoam cup of coffee from the dashboard. He sipped the now cold coffee and once again reflected on the request that was made of him by the caller in the middle of the night. He thought it very odd that someone needed a load of hogs on a moment's notice. If the call had come from anyone else than Father Hunt, who was not just his parish priest, but a personal friend as well, he would have refused. The fact that he was being compensated three times the going rate for the hogs certainly helped too.

The farmer dribbled coffee down his chin as his cab suddenly began to violently shake. The quiet of the morning was now filled with frantic loud squeals and grunts from his cargo.

"What the hell," he mumbled to himself. He dumped the remainder of the cold coffee out the window and jumped down from the semi-tractor. He jogged quickly to the rear of the trailer.

Something had the hogs in a wild frenzy. They flung themselves into the sides of the metal trailer as though being attacked by something from within. The farmer looked on in shock as several bloodied their snouts from smashing into the metal cage. Their continual grunting and squealing were unnerving. In all his years hauling hogs, he never observed such bizarre behavior.

The church side door suddenly banged open. Father Hunt ran towards the truck shouting, "let's go, it's time to roll!"

"What's happening father?" The wide-eyed farmer inquired.

"Just get in and drive. I've no time to explain."

They both scrambled into the rig. The farmer's hands trembled as he steered out of the lot. They drove mostly in silence except for a quiet continual prayer that Father Hunt mumbled over and over.

The farmer feared they would not make it to their destination as the thrashing of the pigs was making the rig difficult to control. He merged carefully onto the interstate. After only a few miles, a lone red rotating light on top of a royal blue car filled up his driver's side mirror. He recognized the Michigan State Police car immediately and began to slow while pulling over to the shoulder of the road. "We got company, father."

"No! Don't stop; continue to the island," Father Hunt ordered.

"But... I will be arrested if I don't stop."

"Keep going! If you do stop, far worse will happen to many more than just yourself."

The farmer looked at his priest than muttered, "well, I suppose we best keep going then." He steered back into his lane and increased his speed.

As they exited toward Belle Isle, and continued up the service drive, a Detroit Police car joined the pursuit. The farmer steered the rig onto the island

and turned right paralleling the Detroit River in the parking lot. The MSP car suddenly overtook them and veered in front of them slowing abruptly. The farmer jammed on the brakes and the big rig skidded to a stop. The DPD car remained behind them. The officers in both cars jumped out with guns drawn.

"Thank you, John. I'll handle it from here," Father Hunt said. He opened his door and climbed down from the rig, despite an irate state trooper ordering him at gunpoint not to move. The trooper was slightly taken aback at seeing a priest, and even more so when he recognized the priest.

"Father Hunt. What is going on?" the trooper stammered.

The priest briefly closed his eyes and whispered a prayer of thanks, thinking once again how the Lord had looked out for him. "It's ok, Tim. You can put your gun away. Everything is fine."

The startled trooper slowly holstered his weapon, after all, Father Hunt had married him, and just last year baptized his daughter. Shortly afterwards, the trooper was transferred to the Detroit Post. The DPD officer came around from the back of the rig. His gun drawn as well.

"It's ok. This was a misunderstanding," the trooper told the DPD Officer.

"Ok, but what is up with these pigs?" The officer asked hesitantly while holstering his weapon.

The hogs continued their frenzied thrashing about and wild squealing.

The driver jumped down from his rig and, with a nod from Father Hunt, walked to the back of the trailer and lifted the lever that had locked the swinging metal doors. Before he could completely swing the doors open, or even pull out the metal ramp, the hogs began to leap from the trailer landing with a heavy thud on the asphalt parking lot below. The others landed atop one another in their hurry to exit.

Once on the ground they dashed or crawled to the river's edge like a battered herd, some with broken legs from the jump down. The herd didn't even slow down upon reaching the water's edge but continued into the murky water until every last one was bobbing in the water, or swimming away from land before eventually becoming fatigued, drowning below the muddy surface.

The two officers exchanged bewildered looks at the spectacle they had just witnessed. "Sweet Jesus," the DPD officer muttered.

"That he is. That he is." Father Hunt replied, as a huge red sun slowly rose into a cloudless blue sky promising a beautiful beginning to a new autumn day

Chapter 50

COLTON ENTERED THE safehouse located in a small suburb just south of Detroit. He was practically knocked over by Maggie and Allison as they each hugged him fiercely. "Thank God you're ok," Maggie said.

"You too," Colton replied.

"Is my brother dead?" Allison hesitantly asked.

"No. He's alive, although part of him is dead. The evil part," he replied while kissing her on the forehead.

"What happened to him?" Allison asked.

"Well, he made a very bad choice many years ago. He chose the wrong path to follow. He has a chance to redeem himself now," Colton said with optimism.

"There is a new foster family on their way to pick you up. I'm sure you will like them. They come with very high recommendations from a very special priest."

"But I want to stay with you," she cried and hugged him harder.

"That is very sweet of you to say, but I'm away from home a lot. I kind of roam. You deserve a loving home filled with a loving family," Colton said.

Allison looked upward into his eyes. "Thank you for saving me and my brother," she said as tears streamed down her face. She eventually broke her embrace, rubbed her eyes with the back of her hands and said, "be careful, Colton. I'll pray for you every day of my life." She then kissed him quickly on the lips and ran to a back bedroom slamming the door.

Maggie looked at Colton, then softly said, "I guess I'm not the only one that has a serious crush on you. I don't suppose you want someone to roam with?"

He took her into his arms, "Maggie, I'm not who you think I am. Sometimes I'm not even sure who I am. I wish I could settle down; maybe someday I can. And when that time comes, I can only hope to find someone like you, but you deserve to have someone now, someone who will love you, and cherish you each and every day."

She held his gaze while blinking back tears. "But I want you Colton."

"And, I you, Maggie, but it is not meant to be. As an associate of mine once told me, my path was predestined, to deviate from it would be terribly selfish, and would cost innocent people their lives."

"But you keep insisting to everyone you're a chef. How can cooking be so, so, damn important?"

"One of the most important events in all of eternity was a meal. A group of men gathered around a table to share a meal and were given instructions on how to save all of humanity," he replied.

Colton removed a silver chain from around his neck from which a beautiful bejeweled crucifix dangled. He fastened it to Maggie's neck. "This was my mother's. She received it directly from Pope John Paul II. I want you to have it." He kissed her tenderly on the lips. "Don't give up on Deputy Toney; despite what he told you before, he still loves you and needs you. He's a good man," Colton said, then turned and walked out the door closing it softly behind him.

• • • •

IT WAS A LITTLE AFTER 2:00 pm on a spectacular October afternoon in Rome. His Eminence and Ricardo were each enjoying a glass of Spritz at an outdoor cafe two blocks from the Vatican. Prime-time tourist season was over, but despite that, the plaza was still bustling with activity.

"Congratulations, Ricardo. Colton came through once again," His Eminence said while hoisting his glass of bright orange liquid.

Ricardo clanged the glass and sipped his Spritz before replying, "He is indeed very good at what he does."

"As are you, Ricardo."

"Thank you, your Eminence."

"Despite the violent assault on the Detroit clubhouse making national news, thanks to you leaking to various news agencies that a rival biker gang was responsible for the attack, no one was ever the wiser that our agency was involved," his Eminence replied.

"I have my moments, your Eminence. You are too kind to say such things as it is just my job. May I ask why the pigs? Always the pigs? I don't quite understand that part, never have," Ricardo inquired.

"Ricardo, your atheism hinders your knowledge. Study the gospels, the answer is within."

"Please sir, just a quick summation, if you will," Ricardo pleaded.

"Well, the demons choose the swine; they always do. Then to the surprise of the demons, the swine kill themselves. And, in doing so the demon as well. If we don't allow them into the swine they will search for another susceptible human host and become even stronger, more difficult to control. Much as Botis did for several hundred years."

"But why so many pigs—sixty-six. Why not one?"

"Botis was an exceptionally strong spirit. He had many human hosts through the centuries and required many animal hosts as well. The separation of his spirit into so many animals made it all the easier to destroy him—forever."

"But why a pig, why not a horse, or a camel?"

I think, perhaps, the demons believe the swine are stupid dirty creatures that they can control, but in the end, the swine control their own fate. Not such a stupid creature after all."

"Hmm, I still don't quite understand, but am somewhat enlightened, I suppose."

"Well then, you have just described a critical element of Christianity."

"What is that?"

'Faith Ricardo—faith."

Chapter 51

SIX MONTHS LATER:

Maggie still thought of Colton, but with a wedding just a few months away, she was thinking of him less each day. Deputy Toney was promoted to sergeant and was doing well with his post-traumatic stress disorder, thanks in large part to Maggie encouraging him to see a therapist. She liked the sound of Mrs. Maggie Toney.

• • • •

ALLISON CLOSED HER eyes to make her wish before blowing out the 14 burning candles on the cake. She struggled for a wish, as her life was so good now. Her adopted family were the kindest, most loving people she had ever known and showered her with love. It was so great having step-sisters. She smiled when she finally settled on her wish. She puffed up her cheeks and easily blew out the candles to a round of applause and camera flashes.

Little did she know how soon her wish would be granted, as just minutes later the doorbell rang, and a FedEx driver handed her new mother a package. She curiously asked if Allison knew anyone who lived in Rome.

Allison smiled from ear to ear. With her heart thumping in her chest she ripped open the package discovering an itinerary that included round trip plane tickets, a hotel, and a semi-private audience with the Pope. All were pre-paid. A hand-written note was included that read:

Allison, I hope & pray all is well with you, and that your birthday is the best ever. I'm sorry that I have not contacted you before this but hope this makes up for it. I look forward to seeing you and meeting your family soon. A gourmet dinner prepared by yours truly awaits you, and your new family, on your first night in Rome at La Fomissico—Chef Colton

• • • •

LUCAS SLEDGE LOOKED up from the podium at the assembled crowd, two dozen of the most hardened inmates sat on folding chairs, a guard stood in the rear of the room. They gathered weekly to hear Lucas speak. Most believed he was very gifted.

This was his home now, a super-max prison in Michigan's Upper Peninsula. He had surprised the prosecutor's office by pleading guilty to all his charges, which included two counts of homicide, arson, kidnapping, impersonating a police officer among many others. He was sentenced to 150 years in prison, and not eligible for parole until he was 90 years old.

Lucas reflected for a moment on the unusual path that had brought him here. He felt no resentment towards the judge for his sentence. Lucas understood that despite experiencing a demonic possession, he was responsible for allowing the evil entity to take hold and grow. He never tried to fight the evil that dined within him, but instead fed it, and encouraged its growth until he was unable to control it. Despite all this, for the first time in his life, he felt a profound calm that was not drug induced. He truly believed it was a lasting peace.

Lucas cleared his throat, "Brothers, thank you for coming this morning. Today we will read from the Gospel of John, but first please bow your heads in prayer, and let us ask God for forgiveness for our individual and collective transgressions."

Epilogue

THE CONTROLLER FINISHED his meal and dabbed his mouth with the linen napkin. He motioned for the waiter and asked him if he could personally speak with the chef. A few moments later Colton walked out of the kitchen and warily approached Ricardo. Colton frowned, then sat in the opposite chair.

"You don't look happy to see me," Ricardo said.

"I was hoping it was a customer wanting to rave about their meal," Colton said.

"I assure you it was excellent. The best shrimp fra diavolo I've eaten in years."

"But you came for more than a meal," Colton urged.

"I'm afraid so. Papa is in grave danger and requires your expertise to keep him safe."

Colton gave a heavy sigh. "I suppose I shouldn't complain, as it has been almost six months since I've been summoned. I'm sure the other three have been busy."

"Oh, they certainly have been, but, unfortunately, all of you are required for this assignment."

"All of us! It must be really bad."

"Yes, it is, as is the nature of the threat. It is unprecedented, actually, requiring all of you," Ricardo replied then glanced about before leaning forward and lowering his voice to a conspiratorial whisper. "The Pope's nephew has been abducted and his captors are demanding a private audience with Papa, and worst of all, he's agreed to meet them."

Colton sighed and asked, "My God. When do you need me?"

"Well, actually, I was hoping now wouldn't be too terribly inconvenient."

Acknowledgements

FIRST AND FOREMOST, I want to thank my cousin, Jeff Wagner. Without his insistence and persistence, this novel may have never been completed. He apparently saw some things he liked in the mini-stories I composed and shared with him and my brothers, prior to our annual deer hunting trips to northern Michigan.

I also want to thank my daughter Danielle, for her review and rough copy of the original manuscript. She was a tough critic, but the book is better because of her. My sister, Mary Beth, was the final copy editor, and if she missed a few errors, don't blame her, as I bombarded her with tons of them. Thank you so much, Mary.

If you appreciated the cover design, credit goes to James at GoOnWrite.com. He is very talented.

Many thanks to all my brothers, Rick, Mark, and Ken, as well as my sisters, Debbie, Sandi, and Mary who took the time to read the original manuscript and offer suggestions for improvement. The same for Tyler Dickerson, a friend and past co-worker.

Last but certainly far from least, I give heartfelt thanks to my best friend, who happens to be my wife, Cindy. Her support and encouragement over the years, allowing me many hours at a keyboard pursuing my other passion, was as unselfish an act that I'm not certain if roles were reversed, I would have been so understanding.

Disclaimer

THIS IS A WORK OF FICTION. Names, characters, businesses, places, events and incidents are either the products of the author's imagination or used in a fictitious manner. Any resemblance to actual persons, living or dead, or actual events is purely coincidental.

Don't miss out!

Visit the website below and you can sign up to receive emails whenever Tom Mohrbach publishes a new book. There's no charge and no obligation.

https://books2read.com/r/B-A-QWLH-LXSW

BOOKS 2 READ

Connecting independent readers to independent writers.

About the Author

I am a retired police sergeant from Monroe, MI.

Writing has always been a passion and hobby of mine. After retiring from the Monroe Police Department, in 2011, I authored a weekly article in our county's newspaper, The Monroe Evening News.

After three years, and over 150 articles later, I decided to focus my writing on a novel. It has been a long process interrupted by other life priorities but has finally came to fruition. I released, "Vatican Vengeance," in December of 2018.

"Cardinal Deceit," is my second novel and includes many of the same characters from Vatican Vengeance. If you are a fan of action/adventure, with an emphasis on action, give them a try.

My chief writing influences are John Sanford (Prey Novels), Lee Child (Reacher Novels), Robert B. Parker (Spencer Series), Vince Flynn (Rapp series) and Daniel Silva (Gabriel Allon Novels).

I currently reside in New Port Richey, Florida, with my wife, Cindy, and our Corgi-Chihuahua mix, Buster-Brown. We have a daughter, Danielle, who lives in Chicago, Illinois where she pursues her passions of the theater and writing.

Besides writing, I also enjoy spending time outdoors, fishing, hiking, and bow hunting.

Read more at https://tommohrbach.com.

Made in the USA
Columbia, SC
14 July 2023